"You're Wrong, You Know."

His voice was a silky warning. "You haven't got a chance. Before this is finished my taste will be on your lips. Those golden-flecked eyes will look only at me, and your heart will beat quicker at the sound of my name."

Tracy cursed her open, revealing face as he grinned wickedly.

He put out a restraining hand as she reached for the door. "I'm going to win, Tracy Maguire. You'll soon belong to me."

"Only time will tell," she challenged. "You could prove to be completely resistible."

RITA RAINVILLE

grew up reading truckloads of romances and replotting the endings of sad movies. She has always wanted to write the kind of romances she likes to read. She finds people endlessly interesting and that is reflected in her writing. She is happily married and lives in California with her family.

Dear Reader:

I'd like to take this opportunity to thank you for all your support and encouragement of Silhouette Romances.

Many of you write in regularly, telling us what you like best about Silhouette, which authors are your favorites. This is a tremendous help to us as we strive to publish the best contemporary romances possible.

All the romances from Silhouette Books are for you, so enjoy this book and the many stories to come.

Karen Solem
Editor-in-Chief
Silhouette Books

RITA RAINVILLE
Challenge the Devil

Silhouette Romance

Published by Silhouette Books New York

America's Publisher of Contemporary Romance

SILHOUETTE BOOKS, a Division of Simon & Schuster, Inc.
1230 Avenue of the Americas, New York, N.Y. 10020

Distributed by Pocket Books

ISBN: 0-671-57313-6

First Silhouette Books printing August, 1984

10 9 8 7 6 5 4 3 2 1

All of the characters in this book are fictitious. Any resemblance to actual persons, living or dead, is purely coincidental.

Map by Ray Lundgren

America's Publisher of Contemporary Romance

Printed in the U.S.A.

To my husband, Don,
who never reads romances but has always
believed I could write them.

NEW HAMPSHIRE

MASSACHUSETTS

ATLANTIC OCEAN

Boston
Charles River
Needham

Massachusetts Bay

Cape Cod

Plainville
North Attleborough
Attleborough

Providence

CONN.

RHODE ISLAND

Newport

Martha's Vineyard

MASSACHUSETTS

Chapter One

"I like a woman who knows her value. Exactly how expensive are you, Red?"

Tracy Maguire stiffened. The voice, coming from behind her in an elevator she had thought unoccupied except for herself, was a shock. The *quality* of the deep voice, with its silken overtones of arrogance, meant nothing but trouble. In the moments following his question, Tracy was immobilized by the fury flooding her body. What the hell did he think she was?

Recalling the conversation he had just overheard, she groaned inwardly. But, damn it, no one had the right to condemn her on such flimsy evidence!

A look her brothers would have easily recognized flitted across her face. If that was what he wanted to believe, then let him. She was only staying at the hotel for the computer convention. Three more days and she would be gone.

Tracy turned her head slowly. Her hazel glare,

glittering with frozen flecks of green and gold, was usually sufficient. But this time it did not annihilate the man. In fact, it seemed to have no effect on him at all. He looked, she decided, like a man who had never been intimidated.

Strong cheekbones flanked an arrogant blade of nose. The gleam in his silvery-green eyes was that of a winter-thin wolf zeroing in on some hapless quarry. Heavy russet brows rose mockingly under auburn hair several shades darker than her own. Her eyes moved down to a stubborn cleft chin and a hard mouth. Yes indeedy, most definitely trouble.

He was wearing a dark suit, the cost of which would have paid her rent for six months. His suit covered the body of an athlete—broad chest and shoulders, lean waist and hips.

An elusive sense of déjà vu tugged at Tracy as she tabulated the evidence before her. A man of power and experience. Not all of it salubrious, judging from the cynical twist of his mouth. A successful man who walked over, not around, the competition. A man who took what he wanted, paid the price and always received full value. Last, but far from least, a man of staggering sensuality. Definitely not one who had to pay for his women.

And if that weren't enough, he towered almost a foot over her five feet five inches. A bit intimidating, she admitted reluctantly. The men in her family were tall, but this was ridiculous.

The sense of recognition was increasing despite her certainty they had never met. The portrait! That's where she had seen him. Well, not exactly *him,* she reasoned, but the resemblance was uncanny. Three weeks ago in Los Angeles. The art museum. The painting was old, the artist undeniably a master. But it was the subject who had transfixed her, held her captive among the slowly revolving crowd. An early Celtic chieftain. A warrior and a dreamer standing atop a rocky hill, his very stance a challenge. A proud man who might meet with temporary defeat, but would never be conquered.

The stranger's eyes swept past her startled expression, pausing with interest on her full breasts, covered, but not concealed, by the bodice of her buttercup sun dress. They flicked down beyond the small waist, slowly surveying the curve of her hips.

"Your mouth's open, honey," he drawled. "And you didn't answer my question. How expensive?"

"You can't afford me," she snarled. Wheeling with ill-concealed temper as the elevator drew to a halt and the doors opened, she stalked into the hallway. Her progress was halted by the commanding voice.

"Name your price, Red."

Feeling safer and thus more intrepid because of the distance now between them, Tracy turned slowly to face him, her medium-heeled sandals planted firmly in the deeply piled crimson rug. She eyed him coldly, from his burnished head down to his gleaming Italian leather shoes.

"I *start* at two hundred dollars an hour," she said stonily, quoting her usual professional consulting fee, "but I select my own clients." Her tone indicated that it would be a cold day in hell before he was among them.

Ignoring the sardonic curve of his hard mouth, she spun on her heel, muttering as her skirt flipped up to expose long shapely legs, and covered the remaining distance to her door. Her fervent prayer was answered when the key turned easily, and the door swung open. She ignored the prickling sensation running from her nape to her hips as his eyes, full of speculation, followed her every move.

Closing the door softly behind her, Tracy sagged against it, her knees buckling in delayed reaction. The nerve of him, the unmitigated gall! He actually had the audacity to . . . to *dicker* with her in a public hallway, demanding that she set a price on herself. And where did *he* get off calling her or anyone else Red?

She looked around the room, which was flooded with early September sunshine. Finally, her fury diminishing, she gradually responded to the soothing elements of the room. It was nicer than most, blending a tasteful array of earth tones. A dark brown quilted bedspread covered the double bed, and a bouquet of bronze chrysanthemums, selected the previous day at Quincy Market, produced a blaze of color that was reflected in the mirrored dresser.

Shaking her head as if she could dislodge the simmering anger with such a simple gesture, Tracy perched on the foot of the bed. After a long moment, she sighed philosophically. Life certainly had its little surprises.

Just fifteen minutes earlier, she had been strolling through the Boston Common listening to the echo of her father's voice.

"Impossible! It can't be done." Her entire family in California had said much the same.

She had continued down Arlington Street past the Ritz-Carlton and turned into the large, elegant, canopied door of her hotel.

"Two and a half months? You're crazy!" Her eldest brother's flat statement had been issued as he scrutinized her for signs of incipient madness.

She had crossed the lobby, wending her way through artfully placed greenery and a clutch of comfortable chairs. Her mother's wail of disbelief had

been the next voice she remembered as she prodded
the elevator button with a slim finger.

"You're committing professional suicide! No one
could do that conversion in such a short time."

Her two remaining brothers had agreed. "You're
nuts," they assured her.

It was neither her slim, shapely form, nor the air of
composure and confidence with which Tracy waited
that attracted the attention of the wiry man standing
near the reception desk. Her luxurious mane of
flame-red hair, falling below her shoulders in softly
tumbled waves, drew his gaze. His lips curved in a
delighted grin and he hurried across the room to catch
her before the elevator arrived.

Sliding a muscular arm around her small waist, he
asked in a low voice, "You're a long way from home,
young lady. Are you lost?"

Her expression was reflective as she turned in the
curve of his arm. "No, I don't think so. I left home
with a compass, plane ticket and taxi fare. I found this
place with no trouble at all." Rising lightly on her toes
and smiling broadly, she planted an enthusiastic kiss
on his chin. "How are you, Jonny dear?"

His hands squeezed her slim shoulders, tanned and
bare but for the thin straps of her sun dress. "Don't
'Jonny, dear' me. It's been a year since I saw you, and
that was in California. Aren't you even a little surprised?"

"Nope. But then, I have a slight advantage. I knew
I was coming to the convention, I knew you were
going to present some of the seminars and I definitely
planned on seeing you." She hugged him swiftly
around the waist and looked laughingly into his dark
blue eyes. "So, surprised I'm not. Excited I am.
How's my other brother?"

The look on Jonathan Trent's face was wry but

persevering as he replied, "Haven't you figured out yet that I'm not your brother? I'm the guy next door. The one all the books say that you're eventually supposed to fall in love with."

"I do love you," she protested. "But you'll always be my brother." Tracy spoke firmly, knowing that the issue, which had been rearing its head with alarming regularity and persistence for the last five of her twenty-five years, must be resolved.

"Sure about that?" His eyes were probing.

"Absolutely. Come on, admit it, Jon. You wouldn't know what to do if I turned into your favorite sexual fantasy and promised my undying love."

"I'd figure it out," he assured her laconically. Her large hazel eyes, tantalizingly tilted at the corners, anxiously studied his own. He sighed softly. "You really mean it, don't you, kitten?"

"I really do," she agreed softly. "Jon, if that particular spark existed between us, we would have discovered it long before this." She linked her arm through his. "You're family. You've always been around when I needed you. You came home from college to take me to the senior prom when my date had appendicitis, you rallied around when Ralph and I broke our engagement, you—"

He interrupted what threatened to become a lengthy recital. "Okay, enough of the testimonials. I'm convinced." Regret momentarily darkened his eyes. "Look, Tracy, I have to check on the rooms we're using for the seminar, and I'm running late. I'll be free in a couple of hours. How about having dinner with me?"

Tracy nodded affirmatively just as the elevator doors behind her parted. Hands once again on her shoulders, Jon eased her back through the opening and leaned a broad shoulder on the door to prevent it from closing. "It's been too long, kitten," he murmured softly. "I'll call you in awhile about tonight. What room are you in?"

Tracy reached in her shoulder bag, muttering as she fumbled for her key. "Nine twenty-two," she verified, reading the number from the plastic tag. "Make it early. I can hardly wait."

"You're really something else, you know that?" he said with a smile, leaning down to kiss the tip of her nose.

"I'm more than that," she retorted with spirit. "I've come a long way this last year. And," she stated with a speaking look, reminding him of the years they had patronized the fast-food chains, subsisting on pizza and hamburgers, "I'm more expensive!" She laughed as he winced and stepped back with a grin, allowing the door to close.

Smiling at the button panel as if the rangy form and mane of light brown hair were still before her, she pushed the button for the ninth floor.

And that was when all hell had broken loose.

That green-eyed devil was enough to try the most even of tempers, she thought, thumping the mattress with a small fist. Unfortunately, an even temperament was something she had never been able to claim for herself. But she had worked hard to learn to control her hair-trigger temper. Meditation, learned from her close friend and mentor, Rama, had helped a lot.

She scooted to the middle of the bed and sat cross-legged, turned-up palms resting lightly on her knees. Her eyes closed. Just as she felt the first twanging nerve relax, a brisk rapping at the door shattered her concentration.

"Who is it?" Irritation sharpened her normally husky voice.

"Bellboy, miss. With a message."

"Just a minute."

An open-faced teenager in a dove-gray uniform

smiled as she cautiously opened the door. He handed her an envelope. "I'm to wait out here for an answer," he informed her politely.

It was an ivory envelope with the hotel logo embossed in the upper left corner. Strange. If Jon couldn't make dinner, it would have been quicker to call. She slit the envelope neatly at the top and withdrew a piece of matching stationery folded in half. As she opened the sheet, two bank notes slid out and drifted to the floor. Her eyes widened in shock at the denomination of the bills. One thousand dollars! Each!

Tracy's fingers trembled as she slowly lifted the note. The succinct message leaped out at her in a bold, black, arrogant scrawl. *I'm in the penthouse,* it said simply and was signed with a large initial that could have been any one of several.

"That bastard!" she whispered in a shaken voice, staring at the note as if it were a snake. Placing it carefully on the desk, she removed paper and an envelope from the drawer and scrabbled for a pen. A few minutes later, with nothing yet written, she replaced the pen.

Her hands fell lax in her lap and she sat with eyes closed, breathing deeply and regularly. Her smile, when she opened her eyes, reflected none of Rama's gentle teachings of charity and forgiveness. If anything, it was more like the glittering anticipation of a Borgia watching his intended victim reach for a poisoned goblet.

The bills were lying on the floor. She retrieved them. Considering them for a moment, she calmly tore them in several strips. Folding them, she repeated the process and dumped the tattered remnants in the envelope. She sealed it neatly, reached for her purse and opened the door.

"Give this to the gentleman, please," she said evenly as she handed the envelope to the boy.

He backed away as she reached in her purse for a tip. "Thank you, miss, but that's been taken care of."

The door was closed softly, with deliberation. With great care, as if a sudden movement would shatter her fragile composure, Tracy returned to her chair. She could easily picture the whistling bellboy entering the elevator and emerging at the penthouse. Smiling again, this time a bit like a cat licking its whiskers after devouring a plump mouse, she visualized the anger and chagrin of a certain very large man. Drastic action, perhaps, but guaranteed to cool his interest.

It was fortunate for her peace of mind that she did not see the hard smile and sudden sparkle in the eyes of that same man as he emptied a stream of green and white confetti into the broad palm of his left hand.

Jonathan raised his wineglass in a silent toast. His eyes admired the charming picture Tracy made in the forest-green silk dress that lovingly followed her curves, but his mind was obviously on another matter.

"Well," he said, resuming the conversation interrupted by the waiter, "we've established the fact that everyone is fine. I'm fine, you're fine, and our families are fine. Now, are you going to tell me what you're doing here? I'm assuming, of course, that you didn't come just for the convention. Or to see me. Are you still with the L.A. branch of SynTel?"

"Yes," she said, answering his last question and ignoring the rest. "I'm still with them. I've had a promotion, and a good raise in the last few months."

"Well-deserved and long overdue, no doubt."

"Well," she strung the word out thoughtfully, then opted for honesty. "Yes, to both observations." She took a sip of the pale, chilled Liebfraumilch, savoring it for a moment before continuing. "As you well know, they're a pretty conservative company and it's hard to make a dent in the male hierarchy."

His eyes darkened sympathetically. "Discrimination?"

"Not really." She shook her head negatively, and he was momentarily distracted by the highlights of her fiery hair. "Not the way you mean it. It's just that the men with power are older, somewhere in age between my parents and grandparents, and their attitudes are pretty well established. The president stopped me one day, actually patted me on the cheek and said it amazed him how anyone as pretty as I could operate a computer, much less understand how one functions."

Jon sucked in his breath with a soft hiss. "How many pieces was he in when he walked away?" he asked with a grin, only too familiar with her temper.

"I almost let go with a few less than tactful statements, but I controlled myself. He's a nice man, and he thought he was paying me a compliment."

Jon waited patiently while she collected her thoughts. "When I moved to their company a year ago, I knew I'd have a battle on my hands. I was their token woman. They were going to display me to the world—and the government with its fat contracts—to show that they believed in equal opportunity. They are ethical, aggressively active in the computer field and as honest as most. But they hired me because I was a woman. I could have been totally incompetent, and they would still have hired me. They needed a woman executive on their staff in order to be eligible for certain contracts."

She curled her fingers into a small fist and lightly tapped her knuckles on the table. "Do you have any idea how frustrating the whole thing is, Jon? They didn't even know what they had when they got me.

But I've been trying to show them. A few are convinced, but most of them still think my various successes are the result of luck, flukes. Damn it, Jon, I'm good at my job! I have so much untouched potential—"

"Hey, you don't have to convince me. I'm the guy who grew up next to you in Silicon Valley, remember?" He referred to the area just south of San Francisco, from Palo Alto to San Jose. The name appeared on no map of California, but was known worldwide as the heartland of an electronics revolution that made possible the advancement of computer technology.

"With parents who pioneered the field, one as a designer and one a programmer, and three brothers who are tops in the field, how could you fail? Even if you had no interest in computers, you would have learned about them by osmosis."

He gently straightened her fingers and covered her hand with his. "Remember when we took those trouble-shooting classes at college that summer? I used to think you were part bloodhound. You could sniff out the problem while the rest of us were scratching our heads and trying not to look too stupid. And then, just to add insult to injury, you'd fix the damn thing."

He watched the tension slowly drain from her face and a smile flicker in her eyes. "Why did you take the job if you knew they only wanted a figurehead? Why do you stay?"

"I was, and still am, impressed with their technical quality. They have some of the finest machines on the market and in the planning stage. They're good, and I wanted to be associated with them. Besides," she added with a grin, "you know I'm completely incapable of refusing a challenge. It's taken me longer than I thought it would to bring them around, but I think I'm almost there. If I can just pull this off, even the fuddiest duddy will sit up and take notice."

Jon shifted uneasily at the martial sparkle in her eyes. "Why do I have the feeling that what I'm about to hear will put an end to my simple, quiet life?"

"If your life is that dull, you need to be shaken out of your rut. Now, are you going to help me?"

He winced as her words produced images of former escapades, all of them starting with just such a simple request for help. "Wait a minute; don't rush me." He neatly cut his tender steak as he stalled for time. "I guess there aren't too many cataclysmic events you could bring about in Boston," he mused. "If you were after the stock market, you'd be calling from New York, and you'd be in D.C. if you were planning to overthrow the government."

"You obviously don't remember your history," she teased. "A handful of men did exactly that in quiet little Boston just two hundred years ago." His groan was an anguished sound. A couple at the next table looked over with a smile at Tracy's ripple of uncontrolled mirth.

"While you're trying to weasel out of helping me, tell me what's happening in the business world here in the city. Who's doing what to whom?"

Savoring his moments of grace, Jon entertained her with the latest bits of in-trade gossip. He was popular and well-known in the city as a result of his position as representative of one of the larger data processing companies, and his connections were wide and varied. "The most spectacular coup of late, as you well know, was Donovan's acceptance of SynTel's bid."

Tracy nodded complacently. "We had a party to end them all when that contract was signed."

"My company could have used the business, but I—and this is just between us—am damn glad we didn't get the contract. Donovan is a great guy, but tough as old leather. I had to soothe his ruffled fur when our company installed some micro computers in one of his hotels and things came to a dead stop a couple of times. It was like trying to calm a grizzly with a festered paw."

Tracy struggled for a properly sympathetic expression and failed. Jon glared as she giggled. "You can laugh. You didn't have to deal with him. I still have nightmares. I hope to God SynTel had the intelligence to bargain for ample installation time and allowed for the snags that always occur. And I hope that their rep has the hide of an elephant, the endurance of a camel, the patience of a plaster saint and the intelligence to run for cover when the going gets rough. Do you know who they're sending?"

Tracy nodded, smiling gently at first, then more broadly at his growing look of horror. Indicating herself with a graceful movement of one hand, she said simply, *"C'est moi."*

"Oh, God," he said piously. "Tell me I didn't hear what I just heard. No, Tracy. No, no, *no*. Wire SynTel. Tell them you've been suffering from some rare tropical disease and the fever just broke. You're not to be held responsible for anything you agreed to in the last few weeks."

"Calm down," she soothed. "I knew exactly what I was doing. I *begged* for the chance. Don't you see, Jon, if everything goes as planned—"

"Listen, Tracy, I'm trying to tell you that nothing will go as planned with York Donovan around. I personally think the man's a warlock. He hexes machines. You should have seen the mess when we installed a word processor in his hotel office. The damn thing *blew up*. And I had to handle that mess. It's not funny," he growled in annoyance as, once again, she was unable to control her laughter.

Tracy knew she was riding a high, and had been since receiving approval to supervise the computer conversion of Donovan's corporate offices. The company, situated in one of Boston's tallest buildings, was the headquarters of his varied interests. Four generations ago, the Donovan patriarch had invested his hard-earned savings in textiles. Irish tenacity and enterprise had done the rest. Each succeeding generation had, apparently, been equally perspicacious and diligent.

Diversification had become their byword. The Donovan family had invested in land, hotels, transportation, oil; the list was seemingly endless. If it was profitable, they were in it. And, Tracy mentally summed up, the threads of the various enterprises blended at the loom of the central office to weave a brilliant tapestry for the stockholders. It would be her job to keep those threads from tangling, while converting from the old system to the new.

The impatience in Jon's voice brought her attention back to him. "I'm sorry. What did you say?"

"I just asked the sixty-four-thousand-dollar question, and I'm dreading the answer." At her look of confusion, he repeated his query. "How much time do you have?" Her hesitant expression drew another soft groan from him. "Tell me four months," he pleaded. "At the very least, four. With Donovan around, I'd be happier with five, ecstatic with six. Come on, Tracy, give me a number."

"Two and a half months," she said briskly. "But I've been doing my homework. The contractor has almost finished adapting the new area. The floor has been raised to make way for the heavy-duty air conditioners and back-up power cables. The special fire protection system will soon be installed and—"

"Two and a half months?" His disbelieving whisper informed her that he had heard nothing else. "Why?

Why in God's name did you agree to anything so unrealistic?" Gone was the teasing childhood friend. Tracy looked across the table at a serious, competent businessman who knew, better than most, that what she had agreed to do was next to impossible.

Her shoulders slumped in an uncharacteristic gesture of discouragement. "Jon, I'm so tired of being treated like a brainless bit of fluff who doesn't know a terminal from a train station. Each time I've wangled a new project, I've had to convince the powers above that I know what I'm doing. Do you know how I spend most of my time? Hauling my male counterparts out of messes they've created through their own ignorance. They thank me quietly, in private, but never support me when I'm bidding for a new project."

She held up her hand in a placating gesture as he drew in a breath to interrupt. "Any one of those men could do this job in four to five months. I had to promise something spectacular just to have someone listen to me. Thanks to Donovan's awful reputation and the fact that he'll probably send more business their way if I deliver what I promised, they took a chance on me." She smiled wryly. "I never thought I'd appreciate the time spent in my office just reading trade journals, but I picked up some ideas that will speed up the conversion. Two and a half months isn't as unrealistic as it sounds."

Touching his hand with hers, Tracy said quietly, "I don't want to leave SynTel, Jon, but I can't go on like this. It's my last desperate bid. I *have* to do it."

Visibly bracing himself, Jon asked, "What do you want me to do?"

"For starters, you can remove the 'sacrificial lamb' look from your face. I just plan to pick your brain. You have contacts I need. Even though I won't directly do the hiring, I'll be working closely with the personnel department. I want some recommendations for a topnotch operations manager. If you know of a good tape librarian floating around, I want the name. We'll need to locate innovative and flexible programmers. Because the data volume is going to be so massive, I need—"

He waved his white napkin in surrender. "Okay, I get the picture. But this is going to be a case of 'You scratch my back and I'll scratch yours.'"

"What do you mean?"

"I'll open up my little black book if you'll come back to the hotel and check out a few of my machines. The tecs were tearing their hair out as I left for dinner."

"Well, what on earth are we doing here?" she asked, perking to attention and replacing her coffee cup with a definite clink. "Let's go!"

"You haven't changed a bit," Jon said, laughing as she rose and dropped her napkin on the table. "You look just like someone is offering you a diamond bracelet when you hear a computer is down."

"It's the challenge," she explained as they walked out.

Five hours later Tracy sighed wearily as she poked the elevator button and leaned against the wall. The indicator pointed to the lower-level garage. After dinner she had returned to her room for a quick change into jeans and a striped, long-sleeved sweater. She had reported to the large room where Jon's recalcitrant machines were located and, after spending the obligatory few minutes overcoming male resistance, she had settled happily to work. While she poked and prodded, she rattled off requests to Jon. Smoothly whirring machines and a long list of referrals had resulted from the mutually beneficial evening.

Sleepily she withdrew the list to acquaint herself with some of the names on it. I must try to meet some of them at the convention, she thought absently. Immersed in the information, Tracy stepped automatically through the opening elevator doors and looked up only to locate the button for her floor.

Her eyes collided with the silvery-green gaze of her red-haired nemesis. The hard smile of anticipation curving his lips and the gleam of challenge in his eyes stopped her dead in her tracks.

Chapter Two

Oh, God. The words, although inaudible, carried all the fervor of a desperate pilgrim. Muscles tautened for a rapid retreat, she turned just as the doors completed their silent closure. Tracy, love, she advised herself ruefully, you're just going to have to look before you step into these things. Stabbing at the button to reopen the doors, her hand was stopped as long, warm fingers closed around her wrist. She was tugged gently around.

"Get your hands off me!" The words were brave, but she quailed inwardly as she looked at his expressionless face. She wasn't really frightened, she assured herself, just temporarily unable to deal with the unassailable confidence of the man.

"Not just yet," he said lazily. "We have some unfinished business to attend to."

Her stomach lurched as the elevator lifted and he

drew her inexorably to him. Her breathing was loud in the confined space as she mutely resisted, temper fraying as he effortlessly retained his hold. A strangled protest broke from her as the tips of her breasts touched his chest.

His fingers laced through Tracy's red-gold hair, tugging in a gentle command. Her face lifted even as her lips parted in protest. "No! Let me go—"

He lowered his head and covered her lips in a kiss that left her gasping for air. She surfaced to find the elevator motionless and her slender frame pressed tightly against his muscled bulk. It could have been a time lapse of seconds or minutes. He watched with a flicker of amusement as she struggled to control her anger.

"I don't know who you think you are, but—"

"I know exactly who I am," he said complacently. "Let's just say that was on account."

"On account of what?"

"How about two thousand dollars?"

"Uh-uh." She shook her head in flat denial. "I owe you nothing. You're a businessman. Moderately successful, I should think," she said coolly, lying through her teeth as she returned his steady gaze. There was nothing moderate about the man at all. "If you do stupid things with your money, you lose it. Besides, with a little patience and a lot of cellophane tape, you can get it replaced by the bank."

"No." He sounded very certain. "You did the damage, you'll handle the reparation."

"I think not," she said evenly. "You gambled and lost."

"I think not," he repeated her words mockingly. "This is only the first round." He glanced at the gold watch on his wrist. "We'll finish this some other time. Soon."

"Wrong tense," she said as she stepped out of the elevator, gracing him with a final scathing look, her lips parted. "We've already finished."

The doors closed silently on an enigmatic gaze that became one of appreciation as the elevator shot up to the penthouse. Those kissable lips had definitely not been curved in a smile of appeasement. If anything, her expression had resembled that of a vixen baring its teeth. A low laugh escaped his own lips. He couldn't remember when he had looked forward to the next day with such anticipation.

The three convention days passed quickly. Tracy attended several seminars and decided that she had kept well abreast of the latest developments in computer technology. Perhaps the hours spent with trade journals and on-site demonstrations were not to be mourned after all.

The relaxed, off-duty atmosphere of the convention was ideal for her purpose. Jonathan introduced her to several key executives and watched with a grin as she was whisked away to company-sponsored parties. Those events were where the real business was conducted. Her notepad soon bulged with contacts, appointments and referrals. She also collected, unintentionally, a group of politely aggressive men expressing interest in her leisure hours. Drawn by the flame of her hair, they surged in her wake, traveling the length of the room. Disconcerted by the attention she was attracting, Tracy was unaware of a silvery-green gaze resting meditatively on one of her more persistent suitors.

Despite her busy schedule, she did not ignore Jonathan's display room. She made frequent checks on his machines. Once, she needed a few minutes to prod a cranky printer back into action. Jon, of course, had not asked her to do a running maintenance check. It was simply her tacit gesture of appreciation.

By the end of the third day, Tracy was tired. The late nights and early mornings had taken their toll. There had been no letup in the agenda. Seminars had broken up into conferences, which in turn led to business meals and late social events. The people she had met were interesting and knowledgeable, but talking with them from morning until night was fatiguing.

Added to that was the tension of never knowing when that maddening man might appear for another confrontation. Waiting for the elevators had become a nerve-jangling experience. She entered one only after a quick scrutiny assured her that it was either empty or that *he* was not among the occupants. Late one evening she had caught the gleam of his hair on the other side of a crowded room and immediately joined a departing group of revelers. Occasionally, she was certain she was being watched. A fine prickling tension in her nape alerted her. Once, resisting an overwhelming impulse to rub her neck, she casually turned and examined the room. "No, nothing's wrong," she assured her mildly alarmed dinner partner. "I just thought I heard someone call my name."

And that was how tangible her awareness of the man had become. His presence in the same room was like a touch. His absence, she thought in disgust, was beginning to have the same effect. She did not know his name, had deliberately not pointed him out to Jon, had asked no questions about him. However, if she had ever believed that ignoring something made it disappear, she certainly didn't now. He was looming larger in her mind each day, even though she certainly didn't allow her thoughts to dwell on him. At least, not much.

The next day was clear. The kind of day that Bostonians, after forty-eight hours of windy drizzle, pointed to with a sense of personal achievement. The reception clerk, bellboy and doorman commented proudly on the blue sky and warm air as Tracy checked out of the hotel and stepped into a taxi. The driver continued a litany on the weather—past, present and future—as he headed into the suburbs. When Tracy admitted to being a native Californian, he bestowed a pitying glance upon her gleaming head and offered a tour of the historical sites. She gently refused, and in a matter of minutes he pulled up in front of her aunt's rambling house.

It was just as she remembered. The long walk leading up to the deep, wraparound, white-fenced porch, was bordered by great expanses of lawn dotted with mounds of bronze and yellow chrysanthemums. The leaves of the maple trees were still green and shimmering in the sun. In another month they would be a blaze of scarlet and gold.

The house itself was sparkling white with a gray slate roof and two brick chimneys. Large enough for two families, it had become, over the years, a sanctuary for all visiting relatives. Well kept, but not fanatically so, she decided. It was a home, not a showplace.

Meghan Forrest, her mother's identical twin, younger by one minute, was a blithe spirit. Widowed when her boys, twins themselves, were ten, she had mourned deeply but raised her sons in an atmosphere of light and love. Tracy admired her youthful, gallant aunt and would have been surprised to know that others saw in her the same valiant approach to life, the same *joie de vivre*.

"Tracy! Darling, you haven't changed a bit!" Her aunt ran lightly down the stairs to greet Tracy with an enthusiastic hug.

"Well, it's been two long years since you visited us,

but I think I quit changing some time ago." Slipping her arm around Meg's trim waist, Tracy waved good-bye to the friendly cabby, picked up her case and turned to the house. "It's so good to be here," she said with a satisfied sigh. "I think I finally figured out how you keep this place looking so terrific. You've found a band of elves who come out every night to paint and do the yard with manicuring scissors. Right?"

"Heck. You've guessed my secret. Well, since you know all, come in and see what they've done to the house."

Interrupting each other with rapid-fire questions and items of family news, they walked up the front steps. Tracy admired the large oval beveled-glass window in the heavy wooden front door. The house must have been built well over a hundred years ago, she thought, and realized with amusement that it was probably older than a good deal of California.

"Have my things arrived?"

"Several days ago. And it took two stalwart men most of the day to lug everything upstairs." At Tracy's look of consternation, Meg laughed. "Don't be an idiot. I'm exaggerating. As usual. Come up and see how I've arranged things."

Waving her hand at several doors on the second floor, Meg said, "I've made some changes and I think you'll have an ideal arrangement. You expressed concern about disturbing me if you came in late, so I put you back here. This way, you won't have to tiptoe by my room in the front. You can go right from the garage to the rear door and staircase."

She opened the door to a large sunny bedroom that looked as if it belonged in another century. The old rosewood bed was graced with a hand-crocheted bedspread and bright yellow throw pillows. Lace curtains and woven drapes enclosed a bank of windows. The charming combination of old and new entranced Tracy.

"That door," Meg pointed to the far end of the room, "leads to the bathroom and goes through to your workroom."

"Meg, this is lovely, but I didn't expect you to change the entire house around just to accommodate me." She turned to the older woman, plainly uncomfortable.

"Tracy, it's been so damn quiet around here since the boys have been away at college, I've been bored to death. You can't imagine how pleased and excited I've been since we made the arrangements for you to stay here. Anything I've done, and it hasn't been all that much, has been done out of love and only because I wanted to. Will you please accept it on that basis?"

Relief washed through Tracy. "Okay, Auntie Meg," she said meekly.

"Brat. Come on, let's go through to the other room. I had the bed taken out. You said you were bringing books, so I got a couple of bookcases and a large working table. Your telephone for business calls was installed yesterday, and I had them put an extension in your bedroom. You'll have to decide what sort of lighting you'll need in here. But first, we need some food."

Thirty minutes later they had finished lunch. After a brief, comfortable silence, the older woman spoke. "Suppose you tell your old Aunt Meg what's got you so tied up in knots."

"What makes you think anything is wrong?" Tracy asked carefully.

Meg smiled. "We're too much alike for me not to know when something is bothering you." Lifting the teapot, she raised an inquiring brow, and poured the steaming brew at Tracy's nod.

Tracy scowled blackly at her cup and finally raised

her eyes to her aunt's expectant face. "Meggie, I think I've finally done it this time. I set myself up for a job, and the more I think about it, the more I wonder if I can do it." Soothed by Meg's calm attentiveness and her occasional comments, Tracy, in her usual orderly fashion, started at the beginning and carried through to the very end. "So," she concluded, "I told them I could do the job better and faster than anyone else in the company."

"You really shouldn't underestimate yourself so, darling," Meg murmured with a grin. "But then, self-confidence is a trait lacking neither in the O'Briens or the Maguires." Her voice grew brisk as she asked, "What made you decide on the two and a half month deadline?"

"I figured right down to the line and added two weeks for emergencies."

"Has anything changed since then? Other than having listened to too many people who've said you can't do it?" A smile grew on her face as a faint gleam kindled in Tracy's eyes. "If you decided you could do it, I know you can. I've seen you in some pretty tight places, but your time evaluations were rarely off. There may be more emergencies, and you may have to work longer hours, but you will do it.

"And I," she announced grandly, relieved to see the depression lifting from Tracy's face, "will be your ace in the hole, your backup, your army of one. Any errands you need run, any calls to be made, whatever you need done while you're at work, I'll do. Oh, Tracy, this is going to be *fun*."

"You're right!" Determination fairly crackled in her hazel eyes. "And with one hand tied behind me, I can handle Jon's warlock, Mr. York Donovan."

Speaking of one daunting man evoked thoughts of another, and she asked, "Did I tell you about the madman I met in the elevator at the hotel?" The two women were giggling like schoolgirls as she finished the story.

"I wish I could have been a mouse watching the whole thing." Meg sighed, wiping her eyes. "Well, you can rest assured that if you ever meet again, he won't offer you any money."

The rest of the afternoon was spent unpacking Tracy's belongings and creating an efficient workroom. Serious consideration was given to lighting as Tracy anticipated the long work hours looming ahead of her. They finally settled on a wall lamp with a powerful light and a flexible gooseneck. As an afterthought they added a fluorescent desk lamp. Several cases of books were shelved, and manuals were placed near the worktable for easy access.

Later that evening, they settled back with sighs of contentment to enjoy a long, cozy chat. Meg poured wine into two crystal stemmed glasses and passed one to her niece with a slight smile. "It's been a long time since we've done this."

"Too long." Tracy thought back over the years and the conversations—no, more than that, moments of real sharing—that had taken place between them. Somewhere along the way, age differences had been forgotten, the family title discarded and a close friendship had been forged.

They sat, talking softly, making plans for the next day, Tracy's last before she reported to work. Monday morning at eight, she reminded herself, she would meet the man who hexed machines.

An orientation day would be well spent, the two women decided, as Tracy would be driving rather than using the city's efficient public transportation system. Her car, a new Camaro, was waiting in Meg's garage. It had been driven cross-country by a young, Harvard-bound neighbor.

It was a white-knuckle trip on unfamiliar multilane

roads, and it seemed to Tracy that the metallic-green beauty winced and defensively pulled in its fenders. At one point, Tracy scrabbled frantically in her purse for change until her aunt calmly handed over coins to toss in the tollbooth basket. The sixty-story glass-sided Hancock building was duly pointed out, as were, a few minutes later, sailboats on the Charles River Basin.

"When I was traipsing around town on foot, I didn't notice all these curves and bends in the road," Tracy commented. "There's no reason for them as far as I can see."

"It's a legacy," Meg said with a smile. "In colonial days, the streets twisted to avoid mud flats, inlets and steep hills. When the hills were leveled to fill in the flats, the streets were just left as they were."

"Oh," Tracy said, charmed. "That's all right then. If it had been done recently, I would have complained to the City Planning Commission."

"You're just a sucker for anything old."

"You're right. If you had lived in California and seen entire towns spring up in a matter of months, you would be, too."

The next morning, Tracy nervously gulped the breakfast that Meg insisted on serving her. She buckled the seat belt of her powerful car, patted the steering wheel as if it were a fractious mare and slowly backed out of the driveway. Twenty minutes later, to her mild astonishment, she was being directed to an assigned parking space in the cement-pillared vault beneath the Donovan building.

A guard patiently explained security procedures. Pale blue eyes smiled at her from beneath a shock of white hair. "Just ask for Nick if you have any problems. I'm usually around." He ushered her to an elevator that shot her up to the top floor in a matter of seconds. Her stomach was still protesting as she shook hands with Mary Silver, personal secretary to the warlock himself.

She appeared to be a perfectly normal person, Tracy thought. A trim woman in her forties with dark, gray-streaked hair, a look of wry humor and an overall aura of unflurried competence, she didn't look like someone who had to contend with hexes and spells.

A quick glance from the other woman took in Tracy's bronze, long-sleeved dress, which managed to look suitably businesslike and utterly feminine at the same time. With a smile of warm approval, she said, "I know it's for Mr. Donovan to do this officially, but let me welcome you. Your offices are ready and I'll take you to them when you finish in there." She gestured to the door behind her. "He'll be with you in just a few minutes."

Tracy returned the smile and sat, waiting quietly. The office was a monochromatic study of greens and was a successful blend of efficiency and comfort. She wondered if it reflected the man or an interior decorator.

"Mr. Donovan will see you now, Miss Maguire."

Tracy stood. She heard a deep voice say crisply, "No interruptions, Mary," before the door shut softly behind her. The smile on her lips died and she wanted nothing more than to turn tail and bolt through the closed door. Instead, pride battled with panic—and won only by an infinitesimal degree—as she stared at the large, green-eyed man standing behind a gleaming walnut desk.

Later, she would take some comfort from the fact that she neither swore aloud nor fainted. Instead, ignoring her woefully weak knees, she crossed the deep-piled, tobacco-brown carpet to stand within touching distance of the desk. A massive desk to match the man, she noted absentmindedly.

"Mr. Donovan," she said, nodding slightly as if acknowledging an introduction. Her voice was cool as she continued. "It seems that before we discuss business, an explanation is in order." It was her philosophy that embarrassing situations were best handled quickly and with openness. Also, if she had the option, her preferred position was the offensive.

A thick, russet brow arched in inquiry. "Exactly what would you like me to explain?" His voice fell just short of mocking amusement.

He isn't going to make this easy, she thought with exasperation. "You misunderstand me," she said placidly. "*I* want to clarify something. The conversation you overheard in the hotel elevator was—"

A look of confusion crossed her face and her words died away as he shook his head negatively. He gestured for her to be seated, then followed suit as she settled with grace in a cinnamon wing chair.

"I misunderstood nothing." He leaned back in his chair, a watchful gleam in his eye.

I won't ask, she told herself. He's just sitting there waiting. But I *will not ask*. They sat eyeing each other for long moments. Tracy had the fanciful impression of duelists slowly circling, occasionally feinting, each taking the measure of his opponent. She gave in abruptly. "Then why—"

"I wanted you to turn around so that I could see if your face matched . . . the rest of you." Even though he hadn't moved, he seemed to have settled more deeply into his chair, watching every change in her expression.

Her lashes drooped as her temper rose. Only she knew the effort it took to maintain a look of cool, detached interest. He was being deliberately provoking, but she didn't know why. And until she did, she would not allow herself the luxury of losing her temper. Somehow, and it hadn't taken long, the balance of power had turned. True, he was supplying answers, but she was being manipulated into feeding him questions whose answers could only be embarrassing.

"And once I turned around?"

"Are you asking if I thought your face did indeed—"

"No, I am not!" She heard the heat in the words and forced the rest out through slightly gritted teeth. "I'm asking why you didn't just drop the whole thing. You had what you wanted."

"My lamentable curiosity," he admitted, not noticeably repentent. "I had to learn if the temper matched the hair." He laughed softly at the look in her gold-flecked eyes. "It did."

She drew a steadying breath, dampening the anger licking through her veins like a brushfire gathering force in the dry California hills. The lounging man across from her, conservatively clad in a dark suit and crisp white shirt, was definitely beginning to irk her.

"And is your curiosity satisfied now?" she asked lightly, as if it were of little consequence.

"Almost."

"Good." The word came with a businesslike snap, ignoring the qualifying implication of his response. "Then we can concentrate on business." The delicate nudge of her last, slightly emphasized word was ignored.

"Before I turn you loose with your computers, there's something yet to be negotiated."

Tracy's nerve endings fizzed with small electrical impulses of alarm and she stilled, seeming to test the air for danger. "My company said all the arrangements had been taken care of."

"This is strictly between us."

She reached into her bag for a slim notepad and pen. Her voice was calm, but the flicker of alarm was steadily increasing. "Exactly what is it that you want?"

"You."

Her head snapped up, and she gaped at him in disbelief.

"Mr. Donovan—" she said icily.

"York."

"What?" She was thrown off stride by his mild interruption.

"My name is York."

"Mr. Donovan." Her words were cool darts of anger that should have pierced his indolent poise. "*I* am not a negotiable item. Your company has access only to my professional expertise, not me." Her tension eased as he nodded slowly in agreement.

"As you say, my company gets the benefit of your expertise which, I may add, is recognized and admired by many in your field." Her tentative smile of appreciation vanished at his next words. "*I* get you." Her breath stopped somewhere between her lungs and her throat at his look of lazy possession.

"Wrong, Mr. Donovan." She jammed the notepad and pen in her bag and jumped to her feet. "You get your computers and another company rep. I don't come with the hardware." Considering that as good an exit line as any, she spun on her heel and headed for the door.

"Sit down, Tracy." He had not raised his voice, but his tone had the effect of two strong hands on her shoulders bringing her to a halt. She glanced over her shoulder; hazel eyes locked with green ones. Nodding at her chair, he repeated his command.

Stiff with resistance, yet unwilling to dump the whole business deal out of his top floor window, she dropped back into the chair. He had risen as she had gotten up to leave, and when he sat down again, it was on the corner of his desk nearest her chair.

"I had a long talk with your friend Trent at the convention. I understand that this job is very important to you."

"Not so important that I'll jump in bed with the boss to guarantee it!"

"Pity," he said, straight-faced, then grinned as her hands gripped together convulsively. "Do you always glare at your new bosses with that go-to-hell-look in your eyes?"

"It's never been necessary before."

"Something's obviously wrong with the men in California." He raised a placating hand as sparks once again rose to her eyes. "Save your fire. No doubt you'll have need of it in the days to come."

His gaze, warm as a touch, slid from her gleaming hair down to her shapely crossed legs and back again, finally settling on her lips. It took all of Tracy's considerable willpower to sit quietly under the sensual provocation.

"I have a proposal to make." His words were as direct as his gaze. "I said I want you, and I do. Make no mistake, Tracy. I get what I want."

"Always?"

"Yes. One way or another."

"Then you've been badly spoiled. This proposal, Mr. Donovan, has all the earmarks of a proposition. If any of it has to do with the job I've come for, I'd like to hear it."

His words were businesslike, but she mistrusted the gleam in his eyes. "You've painted yourself into a pretty tight corner with this timeline of yours. I can help you."

"I just bet you can," she muttered. "And if I refuse your help?"

"You do it on your own, as you came prepared to do. Maybe you'll make it. Maybe you won't."

She darted a suspicious look at the hard planes of his face. "That sounds like you plan to sabotage my efforts to streamline your company!"

"Not at all," he replied. "I won't hinder you in any way," he expanded as she watched him. "I just won't go out of my way to help."

Tracy's thoughts raced as she eyed the self-possessed man sitting across from her. She'd be a fool to turn down a genuine offer of help. And a bigger fool to believe that his offer was other than self-serving. But it wouldn't hurt to listen, would it? Even if he *was* sitting there like a man with four aces in his hand and one up his sleeve.

York watched the expressive face before him and knew exactly when she decided the bait was irresistible. Someday he'd warn her about her less than poker face. His lowered lids concealed a sudden gleam of satisfaction.

"You haven't told me your proposal," she prodded him. He blinked at her brilliant smile of challenge. "I can't reject it until I hear it, can I?"

"So you can't." His smile matched hers. "It's quite simple. We each want something. You're trying to prove to SynTel that this job, in your hands, is a piece of cake. My objective is you. In my arms and in my bed."

Well, that certainly was direct, she thought. No margin for misunderstanding there. "This may sound a bit old-fashioned, Mr. Donovan," she said with hard won composure, "but I don't sell myself."

"I wouldn't want you if you did," he said with a trace of annoyance before he continued. "It is already understood within the company that your project has a number one priority. But you know as well as I do that there's a hell of a difference between following orders and actively cooperating."

"True," Tracy agreed reluctantly. Against her will, she remembered various horror stories told by her associates.

Apparently satisfied with her reaction, York went on in a brisk voice. "I'll change my plans so I will be in constant touch with this office. And I'll make it known that anyone who doesn't meet his or her part of your changeover schedule will answer directly to me."

Deliberately she studied the hard face before her. His proposal was extraordinary. York Donovan, according to the business grapevine, was always on the go. His interests were almost worldwide, and he hustled from one country to another with relentless energy. Nevertheless, she was going to tell him to take his proposal and stuff it in his hip pocket.

"And in return," she said, holding on to her temper with visible effort, "to show my appreciation, I leap into your bed."

"Only if you can't control yourself." His brows rose humorously at her look of exasperation. "I just want your spare time. All of it."

The room was very quiet. Tracy felt a bit like a bloodhound that had lost one scent and was casting about for another. "That's it?" she asked, suspicion rife in her voice. "No," she declared, mistrusting his bland expression. "There's more to it than that."

"Are you a gambler, Tracy?"

"Sometimes. Depending upon the odds," she replied, startled into an honest answer.

He nodded with satisfaction. "I thought so. I'm willing to gamble my persuasive powers against the strength of your resistance."

"I don't think I understand," she said, with an awful feeling that she did.

"Quit trying to complicate matters. I said it was simple. You give me all of your spare time. We date."

She gritted her teeth as he spelled it out. "You know, dinner, dancing, a drive in the country."

"There's still more to it than that, and you know it!"

"A bit," he admitted. "You get rid of all the men you met at the convention, and tell Trent that your time is taken from now on."

"What about you?"

"I'll introduce you to everyone you need to know, explain that you are to receive total cooperation, and do anything else you think will be helpful. Anything at all."

"And then?"

"The gamble starts. I'll use no force, but my intention is to be your lover in the shortest possible time."

"No strings?" she asked cautiously, her thoughts racing ahead. "If I agree to this farce, you won't feel that I've automatically agreed to sleep with you?"

"No strings," he verified.

"I'll be free to do my job without interference?"

"Within reason. I'm in touch with everything that goes on in my companies. But my people are paid well to do their jobs, and I rarely interfere."

"Let me get this straight," she persevered. "The only obligation I would have is to spend time with you. I could say no to your more, uh, physical suggestions, and you'd accept that? You'd use no force to get what you want?"

"You're one hell of a negotiator," he grunted. "I could use you in my legal department."

"Have I stated our positions clearly?" she persisted.

He shifted impatiently. "Yes."

"You do realize that I won't have a lot of free time. I took this on knowing I would do whatever I had to in order to meet my timeline. If it means working evenings and weekends, so be it. I wouldn't want you to think that I was deliberately trying to renege . . ." She caught herself and added briskly, "That is, if I was crazy enough to agree to such a thing in the first place."

"No." His smile was hard. "I wouldn't think that. Your stubbornness alone, aside from your integrity, would make you honor such an agreement. Right?"

Her eyes widened as they met his knowing gaze. "Right!" She would have to be on guard with this one, she decided. He was altogether too perceptive.

"Anyway, I'll be busy some nights, gone others. We'll work out the conflicts." He stood up, towering over her. "Do we have a deal?"

"One last question," she said, refusing to be stampeded. "Are you married?"

"Does it matter?"

"It does!"

The corners of his mouth curved in amusement at the stubborn tilt of her chin. "Not anymore." He supplied the information coolly. "I've learned that temporary associations are more viable in my personal life."

She rose. "Then it's a deal!"

He grasped her outstretched hand, which had been extended in an automatic gesture, and tugged lightly, pulling her off balance. She landed against his chest with a surprised grunt. The sound was muffled as he lowered his head and touched her lips with his. Two large hands wrapped themselves in her hair, gently positioning her face. Tracy stiffened, expecting a hard, demanding kiss, and was disarmed as his lips moved softly, persuasively over hers. The expensive layers of clothing separating them did nothing to disguise his desire, she thought hazily, as his warmth surrounded her.

Before she was completely lost in the heady embrace, she jerked away. His hands slipped reluctantly from her shoulders as he released her. She resented the proprietary gleam in his eyes when he slashed a smile down at her and said, "Your lipstick's smeared."

As she fumbled in her bag, he added, "I don't mind, but it might raise a few eyebrows in there." He nodded toward a side door as he dabbed at his mouth with a crisp white handkerchief.

"What do you mean?"

"Everyone who has anything to do with the change-over is waiting in there to meet you."

"What!" She dropped her small lipstick mirror and looked in vain for a larger one. "My hair must be a mess!"

"It's fine," York soothed, his eyes flaring with a quick, dark hunger as he eyed the tousled mass. He urged her toward the door. "Come on. Let's get it over with."

"Wait a minute," she said, digging in her heels. "You mean they've been waiting in there all this time?"

He pushed back his cuff to check a broad-banded gold watch. "No. They've been gathering for the last few minutes."

"What if I hadn't agreed?" She stood still, resisting the compelling hand on her shoulder.

"You'd still be going in there." His gaze clashed with hers. "The only difference would be that I would introduce you and leave you to it. One lonely Christian in a den of hungry lions." His mouth firmed to a hard line. "This way, you go in under my mantle of authority and we do it the easy way."

"Is that what you call it?" she muttered.

"Well, easier than doing it on your own. You've been through this before, Tracy. I don't need to tell you that each person in that room recognizes the need for change, but they'd be less than human if they weren't concerned about how the changes will affect their lives." As he urged her through the door, he bent his head and murmured so only she could hear, "If you spend much time in Vegas, honey, I hope it's not at the poker table!"

Chapter Three

Late that afternoon Tracy leaned back in her chair with a weary sigh and frowned at the mess on her desk. It was a clutter of notes to return calls, queries from various department heads, and a notice from Personnel requesting her presence on an interviewing panel the following day. The operations manager and tape librarian applications had been screened and qualified applicants were to be interviewed. These were key positions, and properly trained personnel were imperative to the success of the project. She called Personnel, confirmed the appointment, and was replacing the receiver when York poked his auburn head through her open door.

"Pack it up for the day," he ordered tersely. "You look beat. I'll pick you up at six thirty for dinner."

She opened her mouth and, after a hasty glance at his expression, snapped it shut. The tense set of his shoulders and the look in his eyes informed her that he had also had a full day and was prepared to demolish any protests. He glared at her, nodded abruptly, and took himself off with a last warning. "Six thirty!"

She cleared her desk by the simple expedient of sweeping the contents into her briefcase, then turned off the lights and closed the door. If the weight of her case was any indication, it would be a late night. Working around York and his dinner invitation would make it much later than she had planned.

Tracy was still muttering about domineering men who disregarded the wishes of others when she turned the Camaro into Meg's wide driveway and drew to a halt next to her blue Mustang.

"Well! I didn't expect to see you so early," her aunt said in pleased surprise as Tracy nudged open the back door, loaded down with her briefcase, several heavy manuals and a newspaper that the delivery boy had dropped on the back porch.

"Nor did I," Tracy grumbled, dropping the paper on a yellow-tiled counter. "Don't count on me for dinner," she added as Meg headed automatically for the refrigerator.

Meg turned and looked at Tracy expectantly. "Fast work, kiddo. He must be something to pull you away the first day on—" She broke off, studying the taut expression on the younger woman's face. "Not the warlock?" she asked in amusement.

"If you had been born a couple of hundred years earlier, they would have burned you for a witch," Tracy assured her. Knowing as she did that Meg's youthful face concealed a stiletto-sharp brain, she was still amazed at her aunt's ability to reach the heart of matters in a single step. "And that's only the beginning," she said as she trotted upstairs with Meg at her heels. Casting a quick glance at her watch, she groaned. "I've got to be ready in an hour."

They worked harmoniously and efficiently. Tracy pulled a soft amber wool dress from the closet, collecting underwear and accessories while Meg turned the bathwater on and dumped in some fragrant crystals. After Tracy had lowered herself into the steaming water, covered by softly sparkling bubbles, Meg perched on the broad rim of the tub and demanded an account of the day's happenings.

There was a thoughtful silence as Tracy concluded. She had omitted nothing and Meg's eyes had brimmed with laughter at several points. Now they were alertly inspecting her niece's face. "My money's already on you," she said, heroically refraining from laughter, "but I always like to size up the opposition. I hope I get to meet him."

"He'll be pounding on the door in about thirty minutes." Thus reminded of the time, the two separated and Tracy set about girding herself for the upcoming battle. There was no doubt in her mind that the offensive would start immediately. York Donovan would not allow his opponent time to reinforce the ramparts.

She was fitting a second comb in her hair—the style she had chosen was a compromise between a coil and her usual casual style—when Meg opened the door. At the stunned look on her face, Tracy choked back a laugh. "I have the feeling you're about to hedge your bet."

"Tracy," Meg said with feeling, "that's not a man down there, it's the devil himself! He had us on first-name terms within thirty seconds." She watched as Tracy scooped up a brown leather bag and a lightweight jacket. Grinning wickedly, she said, "Remember, I want a blow by blow account. How you manage to stay out of his bed . . ."

Tracy reached for the doorknob. Her hand tightened on it as Meg's bland voice continued. ". . . and why on earth you want to." The thick carpet muffled the sound of Tracy's footsteps on the stairs. She stopped at a right angle turn to watch York as he stood at one end of the living room. He was examining a wall display of photos, leaning forward as he spotted one of her taken when she was eighteen.

He looked different, she thought. Different, but no less dangerous. He had shed his business suit for dark slacks, a soft yellow knit shirt and a leather jacket. The casual clothes only emphasized the breadth of shoulder and length of limb of a man in peak physical condition—a man who had long since trained his body to respond instantly and effectively.

Tracy's composure, already dented by her aunt's last comment, was pierced when York eyed her high-necked dress and controlled hairdo with a knowing look. "You think that will help?" he murmured into her ear as he held her jacket. She slipped her arms into the sleeves, ignoring the question.

York's height seemed to shrink the large room, and she was relieved when they turned to the door. "Good night, Meg," he said quietly. "Don't worry. I'll take care of our girl."

Brooding over his probable method of fulfilling that promise, Tracy found herself being gently prodded into his silver Mercedes and watched as he loped around the front and slid behind the wheel.

York turned the ignition key and guided the car down the wide, tree-lined avenue. He turned at a busy intersection and accelerated smoothly onto a busy highway. He was alert, yet completely relaxed.

Tracy was anything but. She darted uncertain little glances at him. Potential topics of conversation presented themselves to her, but none passed muster. This was unusual enough to startle and dismay her. Normally she was more than able to keep the conversational ball rolling. But what do you say to a man who has declared that he wants your body. Not only wants, means to have. For all his illustrious name, he could be a sex maniac. He could be anything.

His voice came quietly. "I'm not, you know."

"Not what?" Dear God, surely he wasn't going to add mind reading to his already formidable array of attributes!

The creases in his lean cheeks deepened. "Some weirdo who ravishes women in the back country." He glanced at her pink cheeks, barely visible in the rapidly failing light. "Let me tell you what's on the agenda for the evening, then maybe you'll relax."

She resented the smile in his voice, but listened attentively. "I'm going to feed you a meal prepared by the best cook, bar none, in all of Massachusetts, sit you down in front of a fireplace, hold you in my arms and kiss you and then, much against my better judgment, take you home. Now, does that make you feel better?"

Chuckling despite herself at his less than subtle approach, she retorted, "That's a loaded question, and I won't even touch it. But how much longer do I have to wait for this famous meal? I'm starved." Her stomach rumbled in affirmation.

His laugh was a soft male sound. "Not much longer." He veered to the right and followed a curving road that eventually led to a circular drive. The outline of a roof, which was all she could make out in the darkness, indicated a sprawling house. It bristled with turrets and huge chimneys, suggestive of spitted, roasting oxen. Only daylight would reveal whether it was a refurbished gem or a rambling monstrosity.

"Welcome to the Donovan stronghold," he said with old-fashioned courtesy as he ushered her in. "May this be the first of many such evenings."

Sheer delight stopped her in her tracks. A seemingly endless expanse of gold carpet and cream walls blended warmly with lustrous wooden paneling and a spiraling balustrade. Antiques had pride of place among more contemporary pieces. The successful melding of old and new had resulted in a gracious, inviting home.

"How beautiful," she murmured, slowly revolving, trying to take it all in at once. "Definitely not part of the cocktail circuit."

"No. I keep my business life out of my home."

"And my presence here tonight?"

"Definitely pleasure!" She stood speechless before the glimpse of barely leashed hunger in his eyes, swiftly concealed as he turned to drape her jacket over the back of a nearby sofa.

"Martha!" Tracy jumped as he called to the back of the house, presumably in the direction of the kitchen. "I have a starving woman on my hands out here. Do we feed her now, or shall I give her a drink and help her stagger to the table later?"

A short, round woman, covered in a voluminous apron, appeared in the doorway. Her soft, gray hair was brushed back in a casual, easy-care style around her pink face. York's words, Martha's casual stance and the look of mild exasperation reminded Tracy so vividly of the family treasure who ran her parents' home and everyone in it that she smiled broadly.

Tracy walked across the room, shook hands with Martha and introduced herself. Then she asked, "Did he remember to tell you he was bringing someone home?"

"Oh, yes." The tone was grim, but blue eyes met hazel ones with a smile. "We got that straightened out a long time ago."

"I'll bet you did," Tracy replied with a grin. "Perhaps that's the secret. Put him in his place early and keep him there."

"You're welcome to try," he assured her, steering her in the direction of the dining room.

The food was all and more than Tracy had expected, a rack of lamb with all the trimmings, prepared by an artist. Martha's solid presence contributed to Tracy's growing sense of contentment.

Most women would give a lot to be in her shoes. The first difficult day was over; someone had cooked for her and would clean up afterward, and an attractive man—a very attractive man, she amended silently —sat across from her, concentrating his considerable charm on her.

Tracy peered around as she was led into another room. In keeping with the rest of the house, it was warm and inviting. A combination library and den, it had book-covered walls, bright splashes of color and a huge fireplace. For the ox, she reminded herself owlishly.

She kicked off her shoes, dropped down in a fatly cushioned chair, avoiding the tawny velvet couch as if it had suddenly sprouted horns and watched York twiddle with a sophisticated stereo set. Her survival instinct was beginning to assert itself. Weakly, to be sure, but making its presence known.

"Is this where the big seduction scene takes place?" she asked with interest.

The fire cast intriguing shadows throughout the dimly lighted room as York turned. She was, he noted with an inward smile, wary and determined to keep her distance. His eyes glimmered as he approached her chair. The evening was far from over.

"No." His voice was a soft growl above her. Like the anticipatory purr of a panther, she thought fancifully. "First things first. This is where we get acquainted."

"Don't do that," she complained mildly a moment later. He had perched on the arm of her chair, much too close for her peace of mind, and was occupied in removing the combs from her hair. "It took hours to do that," she exaggerated.

"A waste of time," he stated. "And a crime against nature to bind up hair like this."

She looked up and was startled by his frankly possessive expression as her red-gold hair cascaded down her shoulders and over the dark green velvet of the chair. She heard the rumble deep in his chest, but missed the words as she considered the portent of that look. "What?"

"I said, do what you have to with your hair at work, but when we're together, I want it down. Like this." He wound a strand around one finger, tugging gently to emphasize his words.

The glorious strain of a Mozart sonata spilled through the room, softly filling it with sound. "Subtle man," Tracy murmured, leaning back with a sigh, shifting as her arm brushed his hard thigh. Her eyes closed as his fingers tightened fractionally in her hair.

"What did you expect?" he asked drily. Ravel's "Bolero" and a lot of heavy breathing?"

"Nothing so obvious," she assured him, enjoying the feel of his hand gently massaging her nape. "What did you think of the meeting this morning?" she asked, deliberately breaking the intimacy of the moment.

His hand fell lightly to her shoulder. "You're good. I knew you would be. You soothed their ruffled feathers and had them eating out of your hand in less than ten minutes. Your promise of more data sooner, easier access to statistics for reports, and general time-saving factors had them panting to get on with it. I was distracted, though."

"Why?" she asked sharply, mentally reviewing her presentation, wondering what had been lacking.

"Each time I peeled off your dress and had your

hair spread out on my pillow, you said something that brought me back to the meeting," he complained.

"York!" She jerked upright. "That was serious business!"

"So is this." His bland words did not conceal his determination. "That was your arena. This is mine."

"Point taken," she agreed lightly after a long moment, sighing in relief as he removed his large body to the corner of the couch. It wasn't much further away, but she was grateful for every inch of space between them.

The conversation drifted comfortably from one topic to another. To the surprise of neither, they found that they agreed on a number of things and differed sharply on others. When Tracy stated her preference for swimming over other sports, he promptly invited her to spend Saturday afternoon in his pool, followed by a barbecue.

"Fine, if it's warm enough."

"Won't matter," he said lazily. "I use the pool all year round."

Glancing at her watch, Tracy stirred uneasily. "York, it's after ten. I should be going."

"In awhile," he agreed quietly. "Right now, there's still something I want to know about you."

"Such as?"

"How many men you've slept with."

"York!"

"And is Trent one of them?" His voice had lost all traces of laziness.

The quiet comfort of the room had been shattered by his words. Turning to face him, she glared at his determined face. "That's absolutely none of your business!"

"Everything about you is my business." The words were hard, implacable.

"Not my past," she said levelly, refusing to answer.

When he didn't respond, she said, "I wouldn't ask you such a thing."

"Why not?" His words surprised her. "I wouldn't mind. My life, as they say, is an open book."

"Probably X-rated," she muttered. "No, our past lives have no bearing on this arrangement."

"All right," he agreed slowly, surprising her once again. "Just tell me one thing."

"What?" The word was cautious, suspicious.

"Is there a man, a special man, waiting for you in California?"

She stared at him, wondering if a lie would divert him. It might help. But she was a rotten liar, and if he didn't already know it, he soon would. The silence stretched out and she answered finally, truthfully, "No. No one special."

He smiled grimly. "I'm glad you opted for honesty. He leaned forward, scooped her up in his arms and settled back on the sofa with her across his lap. "The rest I'll find out for myself."

"York!" she gasped in protest, as his head lowered.

He stopped with a sigh, his lips just a whisper away. "Now what?" The darkening flare of his eyes informed her that while he might indulge her ditherings for the moment, she was soon going to have a problem on her hands.

She smiled tentatively, putting everything she had into a pathetic plea. "I'm dying of thirst. Could I have a drink?"

She watched as the intensity of his gaze faded to frustrated impatience. His words came slowly, as if from far away.

"You want what?"

"Coffee? Please?" She slid to his side as his embrace loosened. Straightening her skirt, she forged on. "I always have some after dinner. I just can't seem to make it through the evening without my caffeine."

Avoiding his gaze as she perjured herself, she finally felt the cushions shift as he leaned back, deeply filling his lungs. He rose abruptly and headed for the kitchen. "How do you take it?"

Her voice was grim. "Black. And lots of it!"

Mentally wiping her brow with the back of her hand, she chided herself. Well, idiot girl, what did you expect? He must be thirty-six or -seven, not a boy to be satisfied with a chaste kiss on the doorstep.

Damn it! She drummed a clenched fist on her knee. All she wanted was to do such a fantastic job that her boss would beg her to accept a promotion. Was that asking too much? she inquired of the ceiling. As usual, neither the ceiling nor any of the powers above deigned to answer.

York strode back in, a tray in his hands.

"That was quick."

"Martha left it ready for us."

Tracy poured the coffee and handed a cup to York. He glared at the dark liquid as if he suspected it might be brewed beetle juice.

Tracy congratulated herself on a successful maneuver. If this was a fair indication, he wasn't going to be that difficult to handle. There was, after all, something to be said for the Puritan work ethic. Patience, persistence, hard work and virtue just might win the day. She could have the job done and be gone before he even knew what hit him.

"You're wrong, you know." His voice carried a silky warning. "You haven't got a chance. Before this is finished, my mark will be all over you. My taste will be on your lips, my body imprinted on yours. Those golden-flecked eyes will look only at me and the beat of your heart will spell my name. You will belong to me completely and irrevocably."

Tracy cursed her open face as he grinned wickedly and leaned down to kiss her softly at the corner of her mouth. "You're safe for now," he assured her. "Would you like some more coffee?"

She checked her watch and, wincing at the time, said, "No, I'd better get home."

The drive was a quiet one. Neither said anything until York turned into Meg's driveway and braked the car. He put out a restraining hand as Tracy reached for the door. "Just a minute," he said, ignoring her wary expression. "I'm going to be out of town for several days. I know it's useless to tell you to take things easy. Just don't wear yourself out. And save Friday evening and the weekend for me."

Thinking of all the work she could accomplish without his distracting presence, she smiled.

"Don't forget," he ordered sharply, misinterpreting the smile, "you don't see Trent or any other man while I'm gone."

"I remember our agreement," she retorted.

He bent his head, his mood suddenly changing. "I'm going to win, Tracy Maguire. You'll soon belong to me."

She ducked, kissing him lightly on the crease of one lean cheek. "Only time will tell," she challenged. "You could prove to be completely resistible!" She slipped away, slammed the door on an exasperated oath, and ran lightly up the walk to the back door.

Chapter Four

"Mary, is there somewhere in the building, other than the women's lounge, where I can get some rest for a few hours?" Tracy sat on the corner of York's secretary's desk, one leg swinging idly, as she asked the question.

"Exactly what are you up to now, Tracy Maguire?" The two women had become fast friends during the three days of York's absence, and Mary was already acquainted with some of Tracy's more unorthodox methods of operation. "Don't pull that look of injured innocence on me, girl. You're up to no good, and York would undoubtedly disapprove of whatever it is."

Her mouth curved humorously as she recalled the much-publicized, off-site meeting Tracy had hosted for all of the executive secretaries and key clerical personnel. The next day had been the most entertaining Mary had had in all her years at Donovan's.

Managing directors and vice-presidents had trod warily around their serenely efficient secretaries as if the carpets had suddenly become peppered with loose eggs and land mines. More than a few harried executives had called Mary, severely interrupting her schedule, to learn the reason for the meeting.

It had been a rather brilliant maneuver on Tracy's part, Mary recalled. After a short time of socializing and settling down, Tracy had called the standing-room only crowd to order. She introduced herself, explained the conversion she was making, and discussed the effect it would have on various departments and personnel.

Recognizing the misgivings held by many, she responded to some of them in her presentation. The rest she fielded with her own warm humor when she opened the meeting to questions. Her final statement set the room buzzing. It also had the delayed effect of driving a number of executives quietly crazy as their secretaries expressed a determined interest in the very computers they had so recently, and loudly, scorned.

Tracy had stood beside the podium placed on a dais at the end of the room. Her voice was quiet in the sudden hush. "Those of you in this room are the backbone of Donovan's. In most cases, your bosses recognize and appreciate that fact. You could make my life, and your own, miserable by resisting this change. I hope you won't. Not just for my sake, but for your own.

"This is the age of the computer, and now is the time for your company, and for you, to move ahead. I mean that literally. I have never known a key person to be demoted, or her authority diminished, because a computer has been introduced into the company. As a matter of fact, it's just the opposite. Once you understand the potential of this instrument, once you know

how to use it, you will add several thousand dollars a
year to your own value in the marketplace."

She scanned the intent faces before continuing
bluntly. "If not at this company, then another."
Waiting until the flurry of surprised voices subsided,
Tracy faced them quietly with a small smile. "No, I'm
not suggesting that you leave Donovan's. I am advis-
ing you to learn your options within the company.
Those of you who are executive secretaries, find out if
there is an administrative assistant classification on
the personnel schedule. Because in a very short time,
that's what you will be qualified for. If there is none,
have a long talk with your boss."

Letting that sink in, she said quietly, "You've all
heard about upward mobility. Well, that's what this is
all about." She finished with a quiet offer to set up a
learning lab and hold classes every morning at six
thirty. Without exception, the roomful of women
signed up.

Looking up at Tracy, now perched on the corner of
her desk, Mary sighed. She was all too familiar with
Tracy's determined expression. "How much privacy
do you need and for how long? And while you're
about it, you might as well tell me if you're planning
anything illegal." In response to Tracy's inquiring
look, Mary said gently, "Apparently I'm to be an
accomplice. I just wanted to know if I should clean my
desk and be ready to leave when York returns."

"Mary, where *do* you get these ideas about me?"
Tracy chided with an exaggerated sigh. "It's all quite
simple . . . and legal." She shifted to a more comfortable spot on the desk. "Some of the departments are
working around the clock on three shifts. I need to
talk to some of the people and observe the processes
being used. I just want a place to rest my weary head
in between shifts."

"And what would York say if he knew you were working a twenty-four hour day?"

"I really don't care." Tracy shrugged carelessly, but her eyes held an angry glint. "If I were a man, he wouldn't be a bit concerned about how the job got done, as long as it was done well."

"Yes, but you're not a man, and the first day you were here, he made it very clear that he was extremely . . . uh . . . concerned about you," Mary finished lamely.

"He made entirely too much entirely too clear," Tracy muttered, aware that Mary's last words were a polite attempt to gloss over the deliberate impression York had given. With savage urbanity, he had led her around the room, conducting the civilized amenities so much a part of the corporate world. His introductions had been accompanied by a look, a gesture, a tone that declared his proprietary interest in her. By the time she began her presentation, there was not a person in the room who was not convinced that if they weren't already in the midst of a blazing affair, they soon would be.

"How are you getting along with Max Degner in accounting?"

"What?" Tracy belatedly realized that Mary was still talking. "Max? You would ask," she said with a grimace. "He's cooperating, but he gnashes his teeth and mumbles every time he sees me. He hates the idea of his precious accounts being touched by anyone outside of his department. The three keypunchers I have in there transferring his data are counting the hours until they're finished."

"Don't let him get you down." Mary laughed as Tracy started out the door. "Even if his bite is reputed to be worse than his bark!"

"Thanks, friend. I needed that."

Mary grinned at Tracy's retreating back. "Anytime.

I'm here to cheer on the troops. By the way, I never did answer your question. There's a suite of rooms beyond York's office that you can use. It's kept available for emergency situations, and if York hears about this, there will definitely be an emergency!"

The next afternoon, Tracy nimbly descended a metal ladder. She was in a steep, narrow shaft adjacent to the building's bank of elevators. "I really appreciate this, Scotty," she said to the man several rungs below her.

"No problem, Tracy. Any time you get tired of working with those robots of yours, there's a place for you on my maintenance crew." His voice lost its hollow sound as they approached the main floor. "Are you sure Mr. Donovan wouldn't mind your going up there?"

"You were at the meeting Monday. You heard him say that this is a top priority project," she reminded him.

"Yeah, but I don't know that he had this in mind. Only my crew has clearance to be in this electrical shaft. I'd hate to have to tell my wife that I lost my job because some cute redhead conned me into something."

Tracy's husky chuckle drifted down to him. "I won't tell if you won't." She was no more anxious for York to hear of her trek among the high voltage lines than was the man below her. She heard his feet hit the concrete floor and waited for his response. "Anyway," she continued lightly after a moment, "my theory is that what he doesn't know won't hurt—"

Scotty cleared his throat noisily to interrupt her. At the same time, two large hands spanned her waist, lifted her clear of the ladder, and held her patiently aloft until she released the metal rungs. They lowered her gradually, brushing her along the warm length of a familiar body. Lingering for a moment, the hands slowly removed themselves. "You were saying?" York asked blandly.

"I forgot," Tracy said, her innocent expression replaced by an impudent grin. "What a surprise!" Her eyes never leaving his face, she edged to the right, trying to wave Scotty away. No sense in his bearing the brunt of the storm she could see brewing in the green eyes. "I didn't think you'd get back so early. Didn't expect you until tonight." She batted her long, gilt-edged eyelashes like a demented southern belle.

"Watch out," York advised dryly. "I catch cold easily."

"Vitamin C," she said chattily. "Lots of vitamin C will—" Once again she was interrupted. York laid a casual arm over her shoulders and turned with her to face the maintenance supervisor.

"Scotty," he began ominously, "what in sweet hell was she doing up there?"

The blond, fair-skinned man flushed. "I took her," he admitted heroically. "She wanted—"

"I asked him to," Tracy said, interrupting in turn. Obviously the normal courtesies didn't win any points around this place. "I needed to—" Her words were muffled as York's hand settled on her nape and he swung her to face him, burying her face against his chest. His other arm wrapped around her waist, easily subduing her struggles.

His chest rumbled as he said grimly to the other man, "Go on."

"I made sure she knew what she was doing before we started. She's really a natural, Mr. Donovan. She . . . uh . . . well, I guess I shouldn't have done it." Scotty's momentary burst of confidence faltered before the closed look on the other man's face.

"Mmfph!" What Tracy lacked in eloquence, her resistance made up for in enthusiasm. York's only response was to tighten his grip, momentarily depriving her of breath.

The rumble began again, and Tracy stilled to listen. "While Miss Maguire's project has been listed as top priority, she does *not* have the run of this place. If you receive any further . . . unusual requests from her"— his marked hesitation emphasized the fact that such requests would probably be forthcoming—"check with my office for approval."

"Yes sir."

"From now on, I'll hold you completely responsible for what goes on in your area."

"Yes *sir!*" Scotty's rubber-soled boots took off at a dogtrot, palpable relief conveyed with every step.

"Mmfph!" Once again Tracy reminded York of her presence. When he failed to respond, she edged her hands up under his coat and vest. Grasping the fine shirt material along his rib cage, as well as a bit of firm flesh, she pinched. Hard.

"Damn it!" He swore as he abruptly released her.

"You were smothering me." She stepped back, gauging the distance between him and the stairway.

"I wouldn't try it," he advised. The cool tone of his voice was in dangerous contrast to the dark look on his face. "I held my temper with Scotty, but I don't think you'd care for the consequences if I had to chase you up a flight of stairs."

"All right, York." She sighed. "Let's have it. Obviously you're upset about something." She stood her ground, hands resting in challenge on her hips.

"A woman of perception." His words were dry, once again contrasting to the barely leashed anger emanating from him. "You're damned right I'm upset. I'm a hell of a lot more than that! You'd better have a damned good reason for traipsing around an unauthorized, high voltage area."

"Stop swearing at me!"

They stood glaring at each other, Tracy's temper suddenly ignited by his and perilously close to flashing out of control. She drew in a deep breath, forcing herself to speak quietly. "York, the air conditioners are in place, the backup power units are coming, and the main frame will be installed in a few weeks," she said, referring to the costly central system of the computer complex. "The cables are being laid, and I wanted to check the electrical system."

"Scotty could have told you anything you wanted to know."

"I don't work that way. I do my own ground work."

"Not up there, you don't. It's no place for an amateur to be running around."

"Amateur? *Amateur!* Listen to me, *Mr.* Donovan, when it comes to this line of work, the one thing I am *not* is an amateur. If you think—" Her lips closed abruptly over the rest of her furious statement as a grin spread across his face.

"Wait a minute, you little spitfire." His voice quivered with amusement. His next statement, idly spoken, only further infuriated her. "When you get mad, your hair looks like it's going up in flames."

"Go to hell," she said evenly, spinning away on one heel. The last thing she needed was to be patronized by this insufferable man.

"Hold it." His hand clamped down on one shoulder, holding her in place. "About tonight. I'll pick you up at seven for dinner. We can go dancing afterward." He mentioned the name of a well-known club.

"No."

"What do you mean, no?"

"No, I don't want to go out to dinner. No, I don't want to go dancing."

His tanned hand tightened and slowly turned her to

face him. "Backing out of our deal already?" His silky voice warned her to think again.

"No, I'm not," she retorted. "The agreement was to spend our spare time together, remember? I didn't think it meant that you were the only one who could issue invitations."

His eyes raked over her face. He waited.

"I'm tired," she said simply. The lines etched on his face prompted her to continue. "And you look like the wrath of God. Did you sleep at all while you were gone?"

"Some. The days were long," he admitted reluctantly.

"So were mine. I don't want to get dressed up; I don't want to go out. I want to relax. So I'm inviting you to dinner. About seven. After that, the most energy I want to expend is watching you build a fire and maybe some TV."

"Fine," he agreed shortly. "I'll bring the wine."

"Great. As long as it's a Rhine or Liebfraumilch."

"What if I don't like either of them?"

"Then bring something else for yourself." Her hazel eyes flicked over him as he turned away. "York," she called softly, stopping him. "You've got my lipstick on your shirt."

His eyes turned a deeper green as they rested on her soft, pink lips. "It'll be on a lot more of me than that before we're finished." He took the stairs two at a time before her stunned gaze.

At six that evening, a bathed, powdered and perfumed Tracy was standing in the doorway of her large closet with uncharacteristic indecision. Her normal, unerring instinct for selecting clothes to suit any occasion was failing her. After declaring that she did not want to dress up, she should wear something casual. But York was always well-dressed, so not too casual. Another requirement of her clothing, although not consciously acknowledged until that moment, was its ability to stay put once she had it on. York was no doubt adept with hooks and zippers and would undoubtedly be equally facile with buttons. Too bad, she thought wryly, that none of her clothes came equipped with combination locks.

Slowly her hand settled on a silky, green, boldly printed caftan. The V-necked, pleated garment was eye-catching, not too dressy, and most important, she thought as she slowly slid it over her head, there was only one way in . . . or out of it. Adding a couple of gold chains of varying lengths and slowly brushing her hair, she thought about the evening ahead.

York had said he would not use force to gain his end. She was beginning to understand why he was so confident. Experience such as his was not gained overnight, nor was it acquired from books. The deck had been stacked against her when the bargain was struck. And he had known it.

Fortunately, he did not realize the extent of his advantage. Tracy was not naive. She had worked in the business world, fended off too many men, ignored too many innuendos for that. But she was, she thought, an anomaly in this fast-paced world. A twenty-five-year-old virgin. One of the endangered species—and the danger was growing in quantum leaps, she warned herself, remembering York's taut control when he left her.

Ralph, her ex-fiancé, was nice but not a man of passion. At least not with her. An acquaintance of her brothers', he had met her at her parents' home. The occasion had been a party to celebrate her father's latest impressive promotion. A few casual dates had followed and for some reason that had made sense at the time, she ended up with a ring she didn't like and a fiancé who seemed like another brother.

A comfortable pattern was established. Too comfortable. No bells rang when they kissed, no embers remained smoldering to sear them at a touch. Being both intelligent and sensible, they eventually ended the engagement with a mild sense of relief. They were still good friends.

And that seemed to be the story of her life. Growing up with three older brothers, Jon next door, and all their friends, she had been teased affectionately and always protected. Even afterward, when she moved to Los Angeles, the pattern had remained much the same. Men who began the evening with a wolfish gleam in their eyes left her with a warm kiss, a request for another date, and the rueful acceptance that she was not a casual playmate. Initially drawn by her well-curved body and provocative spill of red-gold hair, their libidinous tendencies were dampened by her genuine friendliness and trust.

Never, she thought, had she reacted to a man as she did to York. But then, never had a man treated her as he did. He had all the finesse of a steamroller and the confidence of a man who never loses. He was also arrogant, infuriating, and entirely too sure of himself.

She walked downstairs to the kitchen. Meg had been pleased when Tracy asked if she could invite York to dinner, had even prepared the meal. But she would refuse to play referee, she had informed Tracy earlier. "I'm going out with friends and I'll be back very late."

"Are you going to leave me here alone with him? Throw me to the wolf?" Tracy asked, only half joking.

"Yep. You're a big girl now." She looked back over her shoulder with a grin as she opened the back door. "Besides, this is one war that it might not be so bad to lose."

"Some ally!" Tracy muttered, sniffing appreciatively as she opened the oven door to check the breaded, stuffed shrimp. But, really, if she didn't do some serious thinking, he *would* win the war before she even drew up a battle plan. She was wondering dismally how long clever conversation and a meal would keep him occupied when the door bell rang with a demanding peal.

Not long, she realized, as she threw open the door and intercepted a most unbrotherly look. His eyes swept down from her fiery hair to her high-heeled sandals and back again in one long, possessive gaze.

She instinctively retreated, stopping only when he handed her a tall, pale bottle of wine. Looking at the label, she said with a teasing smile, "Thank you. One of my favorites. How did you ever guess?"

"Just a stab in the dark." He stepped in, closing the door behind him. "I like that thing you're wearing." His hand closed on her waist and he leaned down, covering her lips in a warm, light kiss.

She drifted away as soon as he released her, heading for the kitchen. He eased out of his jacket, dropped it on the back of a chair and followed her. His voice was bland. "It brings out the green and gold in your eyes, and it's sexy as hell." Her startled gaze met his gleaming one. "But then, everything you wear is—"

"Would you like something to drink?" she interrupted matter-of-factly. "You'll have to fix it yourself. It's over there." She pointed to a cabinet. She would not return the compliment. He knew what he looked like and, she admitted reluctantly, what he looked like was enough to make a confirmed man-hater take her hunting clothes out of mothballs. His charcoal slacks and shirt fit like the proverbial glove and displayed to advantage the lean body inside them.

"Do you want something?"

"No, thanks. Most of that stuff tastes like medicine

or," she said, eyeing with disfavor the scotch he was splashing into a glass, "fumes from a bonfire." Pulling a plastic-wrapped salad bowl out of the refrigerator, she added, "You can take your drink in the living room and think great thoughts, or you can sit in here out of my way, but unless you care for burnt offerings, I've got to hustle."

He set down his drink. "Let me help." Smiling at her doubtful look, he assured her, "I'm not much of a cook, but I can manage to follow directions and put things on the table."

Taking him at his word, she said, "Okay. You open the wine and I'll put this on trays." York disappeared into the dining room, returned for a tray, then another. When Tracy entered with the beautifully browned shrimp, she commented lightly, "You've been a busy lad." Soft music poured forth from the stereo, the lights had been dimmed, and the room glowed with soft candlelight.

He seated her and took his place across from her. Lifting his wineglass, he proposed, "To us." She raised her glass slowly, hesitated, then touched his. His narrowed eyes, gleaming in the muted light, met hers. "Don't look so doubtful," he urged. "Tonight's not my night for seduction."

"The last time you said something like that, I ended up sprawled in your lap." The quiet words took a moment to register. He choked, setting his glass down and reaching for his napkin. Her eyes gleamed with satisfaction as she asked sweetly, "Are you all right?"

That set the tone of the evening's conversation, which was precisely what Tracy had intended. She was unable to deal with any sexual challenges at the moment, subtle or otherwise. Their discussion ranged from old New England houses to local towns of historic import.

"Why did you move to Los Angeles?" The words were idly curious, but she realized he was beginning to move in on her.

"A couple of reasons."

"Such as?"

"A plum of a job with SynTel, for one."

"And?"

"I guess I was just ready to make a move."

"You're a lousy liar," he said. His voice held the determined purr of a slightly menacing cat as he added, "I want the real reason."

"Those *are* the real reasons." Indignation warmed her voice. "Do you always treat your dates like this, or do I just bring out your more aggressive tendencies?"

His eyes held hers as he raised his glass. "Are you insinuating that I have no right to ask you such things?"

"Not at all," she replied, forcing herself to remain calm. "I'm *telling* you. My life, prior to our meeting, is my own affair. If I choose to tell you about it, I will."

"Then I suggest you choose to do so, including the men you seem so determined to hide."

"Why," she asked the ceiling, "did I ask a man to dinner who has the sensitivity of an armadillo and the curiosity of Mrs. Krapinski?"

"I have the feeling I'm being led down the garden path, but I'll bite. Who is Mrs. Krapinski?"

"My neighbor in California who could probably answer all of your questions."

"In the absence of that busy lady, I'll have to depend upon you to satisfy my curiosity, won't I?"

Despite herself, Tracy was impressed by his persistence. The damned man seemed prepared to wait all night, if necessary, for his answers. She glared at him as she gulped the last of her wine.

"I'm waiting," he prodded.

"Oh, for heaven's sake!" She jumped up and began to clear the table. Without a word, York rose to help her. He carried dishes into the kitchen and, after Tracy rinsed them, placed them in the dishwasher. All too soon they were finished. Not a word had been spoken.

Having managed to avoid looking directly at him for the last few minutes, Tracy was unsure of his mood. As she watched him put the last dish away, she realized he was not angry. Merely waiting.

"All *right*," she gave in. "There was a man. I was engaged to him. He was nice. In fact," she said, glaring like an angry kitten, "I have only lately begun to appreciate how very nice he was. But we just didn't click. We called it off before any damage was done. No scars or traumas on either side. We're still friends."

Taking her hand, he led her into the living room. He knelt down by the fireplace. "If that's all there was to it, why make such a big deal about telling me?"

"Because you make me so damned mad! You push too far, too fast. And you invade my space."

Satisfied with the crackling fire, he rose and stood in front of her. He placed his palms on her cheeks and lightly brushed the violet shadows beneath her eyes with his thumbs. "Honey," he murmured, "when are you going to learn that your space is also mine?"

Panic flooded her at the deliberate statement, and she stiffened under his hands. Recognizing the familiar gleam of desire in his eyes, she stepped away, forcing herself to meet his eyes and speak calmly. "York, I'm very tired tonight and in no condition to fend off your advances. If you can't control yourself, and God only knows where you get the energy to keep up this sort of thing, I'd like to end the evening right now."

He glared down at her, his voice a rasp. "I told you not to work so hard! But I did the same thing," he admitted with a sigh, "so that I could get back today, and I'm wiped out too. Okay, you'll have your quiet evening," he agreed, his eyes promising only a temporary truce. "I'll leave early so we both can catch up on our sleep."

He sat down in one corner of the sofa, wrapped his long fingers around her wrist and tugged. She stumbled, off-balance, and landed awkwardly in his lap. "I thought you said we were going to talk!"

"We are. I just happen to talk better with something soft in my arms."

"That must put you at a terrible disadvantage in business meetings. Or do you stash a teddy bear under your desk?"

"Brat." He brushed her hair back from her face. "What's this I hear about you inciting my clerical staff to mutiny?"

"Nonsense," she countered, moving her head restlessly on his chest. "I just insured their cooperation and made them aware of their value." She twisted again. "I hate to complain about this arrangement, but your shirt button is digging into my cheek."

He propped her up, unbuttoned his shirt and drew her back against his bare chest. Tension invaded her body at his unexpected action. She unwound slowly, her head resting tentatively on the crisp, russet mat of hair covering his muscular torso. His breathing was even and deep in the silence that followed, and she wondered if he had fallen asleep. The rumble of his voice startled her. "You're making my managers nervous. They wonder if their secretaries are going to look for greener pastures."

"It's good for them," she replied unsympathetically, turning her face into the warm curve of his neck, her lips near his throat as she spoke. "They have a tendency to get too complacent. Besides, they should make the home pastures more enticing."

Time passed as they listened, almost hypnotically, to the soft music and snapping fire. York felt the tension drain from her body as she slumped against him, completely relaxed. His thumb softly roamed the tender curve of her shoulder. "Do you always wear a bra?" he asked in humorous complaint.

"Wretched man." She chuckled sleepily. "You really do ask outrageous questions."

"Well?"

"Yes." She yawned, her voice drowsy. "I'm a bit . . . too well endowed . . . to go without one comfortably."

She could hear his smile as he murmured, "I'd noticed." Much later he dropped a kiss at the corner of her mouth, muttered something about the fire, and shifted her gently to one side. Through lazily lowered lashes, she watched the play of muscles in his broad shoulders under the fine material of his shirt as he knelt to place another log on the burning embers. Nice, she noted sleepily, verrry nice.

York rose, a magnificent silhouette against the fireglow, murmuring, "We have some unfinished business, I believe. I made a promise the other night—" He stopped, stunned by an alien, primitive reaction. The urge to remove that silky thing she wore and claim every curve and hollow beneath it was clamoring in his blood until his very bones ached. He could feel her honey-smooth skin beneath his hands, her long, slim legs tangling with his. Had Tracy opened her eyes at that moment, she would have viewed a familiar sight: a warrior, reveling in the coming battle, fully anticipating victory.

A rueful expression slowly replaced his look of taut

determination as he examined Tracy's drooping form. Her hair was a glorious titian spill against the chocolate sofa, her eyelashes lay softly against her cheeks.

He stood over her, hands on his hips, a dark force emanating from him so that, even in her sleep, Tracy's head turned restlessly. With a sharp sigh, he leaned over, lifted her effortlessly, and settled back down with her in his lap. His brows drew together in a frown. His bargain had been made with a woman, a sparkling, challenging, fiery temptation of one, not this touchingly tender wisp of femininity.

Shifting, she adjusted her position to fit more comfortably in his lap. One arm curved around his shoulder, the other dropped to his waist. Both sandals fell to the floor with a soft plopping sound, and the silky fabric of her dress twisted above her knees.

A soft sigh of contentment escaped her. His hands were warm on her body. One settled at her nape, under the tumbled sweep of hair, the other slowly mapped the curve of her waist. She muttered uneasily as it slipped upward toward her breast. Instinctively, she twisted closer to his hard warmth, moving her tempting curves from his questing thumb. York leaned back with closed eyes and a disinterested observer would have been hard put to decide if he was in exquisite agony or merely savoring a delicious interlude.

Tracy blinked. Something had disturbed her. She blinked again, noting drowsily that York's determined chin was directly in her line of vision. Observing the deep cleft, she decided that it must be the very devil to shave. His arms tightened at her slight movement, awakening her to the fact that she was plastered against his warm, hairy chest with only a bit of silk between them. It was something, but not enough, she decided with a third blink.

"I'm a rotten hostess," she announced in a husky voice. "I should be asking if you want anything."

"Honey, that's the *last* thing you should consider asking me right now!"

Her heavy lids snapped open in shock at the change in his voice. Another shock jolted through her at the look in his eyes. Even in her dazed state, it was obvious that her pliant body had finally roused the sleeping tiger.

He lifted her as if she were no weight at all, set her firmly on the next cushion, and stood up. His expression, as he looked down at her, seemed composed equally of frustration, determined restraint and self-mockery.

"Sorry." Her smile was tight as she deliberately misunderstood. "I thought you might want some coffee."

"Whatever you thought, two hours of this is all I can handle!"

"Two hours!" She looked at her watch in disbelief as he buttoned his shirt and shrugged into his jacket.

He draped a long arm around her shoulders and steered her toward the door. "You dozed off for a while. I would have left before this, but I didn't want to disturb you."

"You must be numb. I really am sorry."

Amusement lurked in his eyes as he smiled down at her. "It was my pleasure."

Words tripped from her unruly tongue as she reached to unlock the door. "I really thought I'd have a chance to rest at the office last night, but one thing led to another and—" Her ears finally absorbed the tenor of her hasty explanation, and her jaws snapped closed. Simultaneously, York's casual hand at her waist tightened, and he turned her to face him.

"Are you telling me that you worked through the

night?" His voice held no trace of humor, lazy or otherwise.

"Yes." The word was stretched out in reluctant admission. "But—"

"You haven't been in bed since Wednesday night?" he demanded, ignoring her attempt to justify what he considered lunacy.

"Yes . . . No." At his impatient glare, she clarified. "Yes, I haven't."

He muttered a short, explicit and exceedingly nasty oath.

"York!"

"Don't 'York' me, Tracy Maguire! I'm gone for a few days and come back to find you prancing down elevator shafts and working twenty-four hours a day. Damn it, woman, don't you know how to pace yourself? I thought—" He stopped abruptly as she muttered beneath her breath. "What?"

"I said it wasn't an elevator shaft," she said, enunciating with sarcastic clarity. "If you're going to bite my head off, at least be accurate."

"You might have been safer there," he raged. "You would have just run the risk of being crushed rather than fried to a crisp."

"Don't exaggerate so; you know there are safeguards. Besides, you wouldn't be acting like this if I were a man!" Tracy's fury now equaled his. She twisted from his grasp, her small fists planted in challenge on her hips.

"I wouldn't have to. A man would know better!"

Infuriated by the chauvinistic statement, she raised her hand to slap him. Some remnant of sanity prevailed, though. A second look assured her that she was dealing with a man who would relish some violent action. One impulsive movement on her part would be like lighting a match in a room full of TNT.

Drawing a ragged breath, Tracy relaxed her taut

muscles. "York," she said in a voice as cold as a New England winter, "don't tell me how to run my business."

"You've got the wrong end of the stick, honey." His arctic voice matched her own. "I'm telling you how to run *my* business. And if you want to get back in that building to finish, you'd better listen to me!" The icy blast of his eyes washed over her, lingering on her tired face. "But I'm not going to talk to a walking zombie. Lock this door behind me, turn off the lights and go to bed. I'll call you in the morning."

His abrupt about-face startled her almost as much as the slam of the heavy door behind him.

Chapter Five

"Good night!" Tracy shouted to the still shuddering door. "And good riddance!" It seemed to take forever to lock the door and dim the lights. Charging up the stairs, she thought about York's astonishing reaction. What an incredibly short fuse the man had! After brushing her teeth and washing her face in half the usual time, she tumbled into bed.

So a man would know better, would he? Well, Mr. Donovan, that was only another man's opinion! Maybe, she thought as she viciously pummeled her pillow, she could arrange to have the entire computer department self-destruct a week after she left the job. In the midst of devising such a satisfying and thoroughly unreasonable plan, she fell deeply asleep.

The next morning Tracy yawned, looked at the clock, smiled at the sunshine pouring through the lace curtains and decided to remain in bed. She frowned as the telephone purred at her. She had requested a muted bell but, at that moment, didn't want to hear even that.

"Hello," she whispered huskily, snuggling deeper into the blankets.

"Tracy, it's a beautiful morning," York's deep, slightly amused voice informed her. "Are you awake?"

"No," she said simply, and replaced the receiver. Eyes brightening with anticipation, she sat up, plumped her pillow and leaned back against it, silently counting. A peal sounded on the stroke of three, and she smiled to herself. Allowing it to ring four times, she slowly answered it. "Yes?"

"Are you still mad?" he asked with determined good humor.

"I don't think so." She was silent for a moment. "No," she said definitely, "I'm not mad." And once again she replaced the receiver. It was true. Her temper often blew in like a sudden summer storm, but it departed just as quickly. She rarely bore a grudge.

Throwing back the covers, she grinned at the telephone's strident demand and answered on the first ring. "Good morning, York," she said brightly, overriding his testy warning not to hang up again. "I know we had talked about swimming at your house today, but the weather is perfect for something I've wanted to do for a long time. I realize that men don't always like to do tourist-type things, so if you don't want to, I'll take my car. After all, Rhode Island isn't that far, and I really don't mind driving. We can meet later this evening, if you'd rather."

"What the devil are you talking about?" he asked in a careful, reasonable tone, as if she had said her piece in a foreign language.

"The Newport mansions," she informed him, managing to imply that he hadn't been paying attention.

"Houses? You want to look at houses?" His tone

indicated that on a scale of one to ten, they fell deep in the minus area of his priorities.

"You know they're more than that. They were the summer homes of the Astors, Vanderbilts, and the rest of the upper crust. But it's okay," she assured him blithely. "I understand that—"

"Be ready in half an hour," he told her tersely. "We'll stop somewhere for breakfast first."

"York, you really don't have—" This time, *he* hung up.

Humming slightly off-key, she showered quickly and stepped into a pale yellow shirtwaist dress. Cork-soled sandals and a lightweight cardigan completed the outfit. She returned to the bathroom, darkened her eyebrows, added a bit of blusher and lipstick, and gave thanks for the clear complexion which allowed her to eliminate most makeup.

Trying to keep one step ahead of York, she thought as she slowly walked downstairs, was becoming a chore. He was not a man to be manipulated. At least, not without effort. Also, he had undoubtedly had too many women in his life who had come much too easily. She had told him he was spoiled, and so he was. Not conceited, she admitted, just convinced that he could have any woman he wanted.

Tracy had already acknowledged that she was out of her league. But, stopping on the last tread, she was struck by a thought. If that were true, then so was he! He was not dealing with one of his own kind, a glamorous sophisticate who accepted an affair without blinking an eye. What he actually had on his hands was a family-oriented type with a small town mentality about these things, and a fastidiousness that precluded a string of affairs.

This, she mused, could call for an entire change of strategy. She had been trying to outwit him on his home turf, and so far her success was nothing to write home about. She absently scribbled a note to Meg, telling her of the day's plans, as her mind buzzed with ideas. Talk about a challenge! It would be a success beyond her wildest dreams if she could nudge him from his current position to the ranks of the brotherhood.

She stepped out on the sunlit porch just as he drove up in a black Ferrari. They were two of a kind, she thought as he opened the door and walked toward her. Dangerous! Dark slacks and a knit shirt emphasized his muscular length and breadth of shoulder, drawing her gaze and holding it despite her intentions to remain untouched by him.

"Do you have one for each day?" she teased, nodding at the gleaming car.

"Not quite," he said absently, his eyes openly admiring as they covered her in a quick, silvery glance. He helped her into the bucket seat, and the door closed with the muted thunk of an expensive car. Within minutes they were seated at the table of a small restaurant converted from an old house. The wide-planked floors shone with wax, and the lead glass windows looked out over a field of tall grass and wildflowers.

After they ordered, he reached for her hand, holding it until she looked at him. "I'm sorry about last night," he said with a sincerity that disarmed her.

"And so you should be," she forced herself to say lightly as she attempted to remove her hand from his grasp.

"Does that mean I'm still in the doghouse?" he asked with a whimsical smile.

"No, it means that I don't quite understand what happened, but I accept your apology." His fingers circled her wrist, holding it still. It was not a painful grip, but she knew she would not withdraw her hand until he chose to let her do so. She concentrated instead on his expressionless face.

He grinned suddenly. "I thought you were going to slug me last night."

"I almost did," she admitted, amusement brightening her eyes.

"Why didn't you?" It wasn't an idle question; he really wanted to know.

"Because you looked . . . I don't know, almost as if you *wanted* me to. I didn't trust you."

"You were right. If you had slapped me, all hell would have broken loose." His face was grim, and she was suddenly very relieved that she had not given in to the almost overwhelming temptation.

"What would you have done?" she asked, almost frightened by his expression.

"I don't know." His voice was tight. "It was a pretty explosive situation. Both of us were exhausted and short-fused. Believe it or not, I'm normally a fairly even-tempered man." He laughed shortly at her raised eyebrows and look of utter disbelief. "But I'll tell you something, Tracy Maguire. I have never known a woman who could infuriate me with a mere look the way you do." She preferred his lack of expression, she decided. The look he wore now said that he had decided he would whip something into shape, and she had the sinking feeling that she was the "something."

"York," she said in the small silence that followed, "we really need to discuss a couple of things."

"Go ahead," he replied evenly, leaning back as the waitress set their breakfast before them.

"It's about our arrangement," she began hesitantly.

His voice was hard. "You agreed to the terms, and I'm holding you to them."

"I'm not trying to change things," she said, refusing

to be intimidated. "I'm attempting to explain something."

"Go on." He was not encouraging.

Toying with her omelet as she lined up her muddled thoughts, she looked up and caught his enigmatic gaze. "I've never had to deal with this sort of situation before. . . . I guess I've never thought about it, and I'm a little confused."

He bit into a piece of toast, watching as her expressive face reflected her inner turmoil.

"Go on," he repeated, more gently.

"When we made our bargain, there were actually three people involved. You, and the two sides of Tracy Maguire." She held up her hand as he drew in a breath. "No, wait a minute. Both sides of me agreed to the bargain, but that's what you have to understand."

She had his full attention now. His green eyes darkened with concentration. "Outside of work, I am one person, ready to have fun, to enjoy your company . . . and to foil your attempts to lure me into bed. But when I am at work," her voice sharpened, "I am a *professional*. You know my qualifications. Make no mistake about it, I know my job." Her next words were lightly edged with warning. "Don't equate my femininity with inadequacy, York."

She ran a hand through her hair, carefully phrasing her next words. "We need to have the same working relationship that you would offer my male counterparts. I appreciate your instinctive courtesies, such as opening doors and lifting heavy objects. I'm not talking about things like that. I'm talking about making decisions and trusting my knowledge in the myriad of details involved in my job. You can't bawl me out in front of someone who is helping me do that job. If you have so little confidence in me, how are they going to react the next time I ask for help?"

She ignored his taut expression, knowing it would only get worse. "Yesterday, with Scotty, for example. I knew the potential danger. But the bottom line is that I probably know a lot more about what goes on in that shaft than you do." She drew a deep breath, allowing her eyes to plead, as she spoke with desperate sincerity. "If you have any doubts about my qualifications, York, contact my company. If you don't, then for God's sake, trust me! I don't take unnecessary risks. Basically, I'm a very conservative person."

She reached for her coffee with a hand that trembled slightly, waiting. She had gambled everything on one roll of the dice and the question was, had she won or lost?

York set his fork carefully on the plate. "You haven't eaten your breakfast," he reminded her. Waiting until she bit into a blueberry muffin, he said, "You're right. I wouldn't have interfered or reacted as I did yesterday with a man. When I look at you, I see a woman—smaller and more fragile than I am—and I want to protect you. I badly mishandled that situation yesterday, and I'll have a talk with Scotty."

Tracy choked on a mouthful of coffee. "You always manage to surprise me," she said at last, wiping her eyes with a napkin.

"And I do trust you." He grinned at her hopeful expression. "But only because I had you checked up one side and down the other when I heard they were sending me a woman." He laughed outright at her glare. "I have to admit, though, that I react to your face and body long before I remember your intellectual capabilities."

His words came slowly, as if he too was confronted with a new situation. "After I cooled down last night, I realized that I was tying your hands and that if I kept it up, the job would never be done." His voice was incisive as he concluded, "You'll get the freedom you need. My door will be open if you want anything. Aside from that, you'll be on your own. I suggest that you join the weekly meetings I have with my managers to report your progress. It's an open forum where problems are aired, assistance requested, whatever. Anything goes, with no recriminations." Her silence seemed to disturb him. "Well?" he demanded.

Tracy looked up, dazzling him with a thousand-watt smile.

"Well." This time, the word was drawn out in appreciation.

"Don't get carried away," she advised with another smile. "I just caught my first real glimpse of York Donovan, businessman, and I liked it."

The drive to Newport was brief and scenic. Accustomed as she was to the dryness of Southern California in September, Tracy was entranced with the springlike greenness of the trees and rolling hills. "Except for the big cities, it seems like someone just scooped a section out of the forest and placed a town in it, then a little further down the road, did it again," she said with contentment.

"Maybe we'll make an Easterner out of you yet," York commented idly.

Soon they were caught in the weekend traffic, and York wound carefully through narrow streets. He didn't drive aggressively, Tracy noted with approval as he patiently avoided the unexpected maneuvers of lost tourists. They stopped at the chamber of commerce office where they rented a driving tour cassette and purchased tickets to view some of the homes.

Seven hours later, windblown and tired, they dropped into the comfortable seats of the Ferrari. "There's just too much to see here in one day," Tracy complained.

Newport's "summer cottages" were, in actuality,

turn-of-the-century mansions whose opulence staggered Tracy. Rosecliff, their first stop, had been fashioned after Marie Antoinette's Grand Trianon at Versailles. It boasted a ballroom forty by eighty feet, exquisite antique furnishings from the Louis XV and XVI eras, handpainted washbasins, and detailed sculptures from the sixteenth and seventeenth centuries.

Parking the car near Easton's Beach, they had strolled along the famous Cliff Walk that skirted the bluffs and looked to the back of many of the magnificent estates. York's arm, casually draped around Tracy's shoulder, held her against his warmth, shielding her from the brisk Atlantic breeze.

The Breakers, summer home of the Cornelius Vanderbilt family, was their last stop. Tracy had a vague idea of what was coming when she viewed the ornate wrought-iron gates, standing thirty feet high, which barred the main entrance. Boasting over fifty rooms, it was the largest, most elaborate home in Newport, and her mind was still sorting out superlatives two hours later as they walked to the parking lot.

"Well, what do you think of the summer cottages of the superrich now?" he asked after flicking several glances at her bemused expression.

"They're nothing like the collapsing tents and crowded campers that I spent my summers in," she said, smiling at the memories.

"I'll bet you had more fun." His smile was companionable.

"I always had fun with my family, wherever we were."

"Do you miss them?" he asked, startled at her wistful tone.

"I always miss them."

"Then why did you move so far away?"

Chafing a bit at his interest, she forced herself to

answer honestly. The only way he would ever think of her as more than a female to be bedded, she reminded herself, was if she allowed him to meet the inner person, the real Tracy.

"One of the things they taught me was to work hard for what I wanted. They knew my dreams probably wouldn't be realized within a few blocks of the homestead, so they taught me to fly and prepared me to leave the nest."

"Clever parents," he said thoughtfully.

Her voice was warm. "They're wonderful. You'd like them," she astonished herself by adding. The heat inside the car made her drowsy, and it wasn't until they pulled up before York's house that she realized how much she had told him of her parents, her three brothers and her life-style.

"What are we doing here?" she asked in surprise. "I thought you were taking me home."

He turned off the ignition, glanced at her puzzled face, and silently went around to open her door.

"York!" she protested. "I'm a mess. I feel like I've been pulled backward through a field of tumbleweeds. I can't go in your house looking like this."

His determined gaze drifted over her. "Right now, you're on a mission of mercy. You can't be concerned about such frivolous things."

"I don't remember volunteering for any mission," she grumbled, allowing him to close the door behind her.

"I volunteered you."

"Well, I don't remember joining the army either," she assured him, leaning back against the car to look up at him.

He grabbed her hand and urged her up the walk, saying the last thing she expected. "It's Martha."

"Martha?" she repeated stupidly. "Is she sick?"

"No, but *I* will be if we don't get in there soon. She

threatened to leave me if I didn't start bringing people home for dinner. Says she's tired of cooking meals that aren't eaten, that she'll go cook for a hotel . . . or an orphanage." He led her through the front door, slamming it and shouting for Martha at the same time. "Just as I promised," he said as that small woman appeared in the doorway. "Two for dinner."

"It's a good thing it won't be ready for a while," she commented dryly, eyeing their sun-flushed skin and windblown hair. "What did he do," she asked Tracy, "make you run behind the car?"

Tracy was amused once again at how easily the woman relegated the overwhelming man at her side to the ranks of boyhood. It was an affectionate game, she realized, and recognized as such by both players. She knew with certainty that few people would see this side of York Donovan, and that triggered a small cautionary alarm within her. For a man who had vowed to get her into bed as fast as he could, he was being altogether too folksy, charming and non-threatening. She'd have to think about it later, though, for Martha was waiting for an answer.

Smiling, she shook her head negatively. "His usual tactics are to push or prod me. I don't think he trusts me to follow."

"With good reason," he growled. "That red hair is a clear warning—"

"Yes, yes," Martha cut in on what promised to be a lengthy and possibly heated discussion. "Right now, what she needs is a shower and a change of clothes so she can relax and enjoy my dinner." Neatly edging York aside with an elbow, she shooed Tracy upstairs.

"This," she said, ushering Tracy into a pale yellow, delightfully feminine room, "is Jean's room when she visits. York's sister," she explained, noting the confused look on Tracy's face. "Hasn't the man told you anything about his family?" she asked in exasperation.

"No."

"A brother Michael, sister Jean, mother died fifteen years ago, father living in Cape Cod," Martha enumerated· quickly as she opened the closet door. She pulled out a jade wraparound skirt and a matching blouse with a scoop neck and long flowing sleeves gathered at the wrist. "Jean is a lovely girl and would want you to use anything you need to be comfortable," she said, aware of Tracy's doubt. "You're about the same size, but this style should cover any differences." She pointed a finger. "Shower in there; a hair dryer is in a drawer if you want to wash your hair. You've got about an hour, so take your time. Don't let York rush you."

Tracy looked up sharply at the last comment, but Martha's expression had not changed, showing only concern for her comfort.

Taking Martha at her word, Tracy let the hot water stream down over her. Luxuriously lathering her hair with shampoo and her body with a fragrant liquid soap, she slowly turned and twisted, her tension disappearing along with the soap bubbles. She recalled her earlier flicker of alarm—and recognized it for what it was. York had created a second front in his battle. Not content to rely solely on his powers of persuasion, he was trying to soften her with glimpses of another York Donovan. If the one couldn't intimidate, manipulate, or sway her, then the other could possibly charm her. And, damn it, she thought, it had been working!

Today he had been the perfect companion. Although he could never rid himself entirely of his lean strength and grace, he had tamped down considerably his sensual charm. Several times, his eyes, lit with amusement, had met hers in silent communication when they had overheard something funny. His sense of humor matched hers; they enjoyed the same things. And he also made her feel intensely feminine and desirable.

It would be far safer to remain ignorant of that side of him, though. She could protect herself better in the clinches, no pun intended, she assured herself, if she could continue to think of him as the arrogant chauvinist sitting behind a half acre of walnut desk.

Squeezing the last bit of water out of her hair, Tracy eased her dripping body out of the shower. She wrapped one thick yellow towel turban-style around her head and dried with a second one. Her wispy pants and bra were on the tiled counter, and she reluctantly stepped back into them. The dryer was just where Martha had said it would be. It usually took a good twenty minutes to dry her thick mane but, thanks to the natural wave, she didn't have to bother styling it.

She stood facing the mirror, more out of habit than necessity. Her eyes closed as the warm flow of air enveloped her. Finally, in response to her protesting arm muscles, she lowered the dryer and laced her fingers through the tumbled mass of waves. It was dry enough, she concluded. Her lids lifted slowly at first, then flew wide open. Stunned, she encountered in the mirror the devouring stare of the man behind her.

He filled the doorway, his stance indicating that he had been there for some time. The desire radiating from him was almost palpable. Tracy's own feelings were a tumultuous mixture of anger at having her privacy invaded and embarrassment at being caught in next to nothing. Assuring herself that she appeared on the beach in no more than she was presently wearing was not comforting.

Nor was his silent regard. She experienced much

the same feeling as she had the night before when she had almost slapped him. He was spoiling for action. One impulsive move on her part would trigger an explosive reaction, one she wasn't yet prepared to deal with. She bravely held his eyes in the mirror as she felt the impact of his presence fill the room, pressing her against the tiled sink.

Willing her voice to remain cool and eyeing his showered, shaved and immaculately dressed person, she said lightly, "You obviously don't waste any time."

"I don't," he agreed, his voice a velvety rasp that was a seduction in itself.

Uncomfortably aware of his heated regard, she forced herself to continue easily. "I won't be ready for a few minutes. Why don't I meet you downstairs?"

He watched her soft lips move, but for all the effect her words had, she could have remained silent. He reached for her, grim and intent, and her voice rose a notch. "No, York!"

"Yes, Tracy," he mocked softly as he turned her, pulling her against his hard frame. "I've been waiting all day for this." He lowered his head, resting his lips in the hollow above her collarbone. "Mmm, you smell like a garden of wildflowers."

"Your sister's bath powder!" she said, twitching her shoulder to evade the seeking lips that were traveling in a direct line to her breast.

"You're so soft and slim," he muttered, oblivious to her words. His hands followed the intriguing indentation of her waist, moved down the flare of her hips and softly cupped the enticing curve of her bottom. Lifting her easily, he pulled her close against his muscular frame, making her aware of his arousal.

"Exercise!" she said, striving for a controlled voice. "That's the secret. Aerobic dancing and jazz—"

"Shut up, Tracy," he ground out softly, silencing

her and taking advantage of her parted lips at the same time. His tongue softly explored the sweet darkness of her mouth as one hand rose to her nape, his fingers twining in her hair, holding her head captive. His other arm angled down across her hips, keeping her close to his taut body.

I won't let him do this to me, she raged internally, jerking as his tongue found hers and engaged it in an age-old battle. It's nothing more than a challenge to him, and I refuse to give him the satisfaction of adding me to the list of women who have eased in and out of his life.

But refusing was easier said than done. The intensity of his silent demand enveloped her. Interwoven with the strength of his desire, it was a potent summons.

Using the only weapon at her disposal, she forced herself to be passive. Her hands, which had shot to his shoulders for balance, then stiffened in protest, were *willed* to rest. She stilled under his touch, mentally removing herself from his arms, using one of Rama's exercises. Picturing herself beside a mountain stream, she visualized the clear water flowing smoothly over shining stones. . . .

He lifted his head, and she quailed at the fury blazing in his eyes. "By God, when I have you in my arms, I want *all* of you, not some lifeless shell!" He bent his head, and his teeth closed gently on her full lower lip. At the same time, he slid her down his body until her toes touched the floor. His hand smoothed its way from her hip to her breast, his thumb grazing over her nipple.

"No!" Her soft cry was drowned by the brisk rapping of knuckles on the bedroom door. "Tracy! Ten minutes until dinner," Martha called.

York lifted his head but did not release her. "Okay, Martha. Thanks," she responded slowly. She shivered at the message York's thumb was transmitting to her entire network of feminine nerve endings. Stiffening, but unable to conceal the tremors rippling through her body, she demanded in a husky whisper, "Let me go, York."

"Kiss me," he commanded, and waited until she slowly raised her gaze to his. Expecting an urgent, draining kiss, she was stunned by the warm, sweet touch of his lips, vaguely aware that his hands were now gently soothing her back in long smooth strokes.

When he released her, she was surprised to see a flicker of concern in his eyes. He drew in a deep breath as if to say something, then turned and left without a word.

Chapter Six

Tracy's knuckles shone whitely as she gripped the telephone. "Look, Charlie," she said, temper tightening her husky voice. "I know mistakes happen, but I thought I'd get better service from you. I have over a hundred word processors in the receiving department that I can't use. The printers you sent may be fine for home computers, but Donovan's standards, as you well know, are just a tad higher. I ordered letter-quality printers, and that's what I want. Now!"

She listened to the apologetic voice until it ran down. "No," she replied softly, "I don't expect miracles. I expect *service*. Before closing time today, I expect you to have a truck here to pick up these printers. On that same truck, I expect to see at least half of the letter-quality printers that I ordered. By Wednesday, at the latest, I expect to see the rest of them. That's what I *expect!*" By the time she finished, she could almost feel him flinching at the repetition of the word he had so lightly used.

Refusing herself the indulgence of slamming down the receiver, she replaced it carefully and sat back with a sigh.

"Whooee, lady, when you get your dander up, it's really up!"

Tracy turned at the familiar sound of Mary's voice, her hazel eyes still bright with anger. "That's only the beginning," she assured her.

The secretary stood in the doorway. "In that case, I won't come in. York just called. He'll be in late this afternoon and wants you to meet him at his house for dinner tonight. About seven."

"Mary!" Tracy called to the retreating woman. Then she leaned back in her chair, not sure how to proceed once the secretary sat down across from her.

Mary finally broke the silence. "Are you worried about the printers?"

"No," Tracy replied absently. "My problem is well over six feet and walks around as if he owns the world."

"Ah!"

"Exactly." Her voice was dry. "What can you tell me about his divorce?"

"I've been with him for six years and it happened about two years before my time. But I can tell you what I learned through the grapevine, and I won't be violating a confidence."

They smiled in perfect accord.

"She was a gorgeous brunette," Mary said thoughtfully, "and York was dazzled. Within six months of their marriage, he realized that she was a first-class bitch and that what she was enchanted with was his money. The divorce was lengthy and bitter. It was a very expensive lesson for him. And, if York is anything, he's a fast learner."

"That he is!"

"Actually," Mary seemed to be treading carefully, "I'm hoping that you'll be the one to end the parade of females I send flowers to and—"

"No, he made it quite clear that I was a challenge to relieve the boredom in his life—temporarily. Anyway, I wouldn't take him if he was served on a gold plate with my favorite bottle of wine!"

"Sure," Mary agreed with an annoying grin as she rose. "I've got to get back to my desk."

Tracy nodded her thanks and absently dialed the warehouse. She explained briefly about the pickup and partial delivery. Then she thoughtfully replaced the receiver.

Two weeks had passed since that last evening at York's home. As if watching a rerun, she recalled how she had stared in bemusement at the bedroom door closing behind him. Still stunned, she had buttoned the jade blouse and secured the skirt around her narrow waist with fingers that trembled. Sitting at the dressing table, brushing her hair in long, soothing strokes, she regained her composure before opening the door and descending the stairs.

She heard in rapid succession a sharp question, a savage oath and the slam of the telephone. York met her at the bottom of the stairs with a black scowl and the news that he had to leave for Australia that night.

Dinner had been delicious, and York had maintained a determined stream of casual observations about her progress at work. More than willing to extend that topic of conversation, she'd said, "There's something I don't understand." At his look of inquiry, she continued. "You really should have switched over to your own computer setup a long time ago. Your work has been farmed out to different data processing companies for several years now. You've managed to keep up with things, but just barely.

Surely you've been advised to change over long before this. Why did you wait so long?"

"You want the real reason?"

"Of course."

"I hate the damn things. And I don't trust them." He grinned at her stunned look of outrage, then held out his hands in a gesture of peace as she leaped to the defense of her precious equipment.

Amusement sparkled in her eyes and she finally broke out in a husky laugh. "I can't believe it," she said between giggles. "York Donovan, entrepreneur, the man who's always two jumps ahead of everyone else—"

"What can I say?" The smile remained on his face as he accepted her teasing.

"How can you possibly hate computers?" Her fascinated gaze informed him that he might as well have declared membership in the Flat Earth Society.

"Easily," he assured her, leaning back as Martha placed large plates of steaming, savory food before them.

"But—"

"I've heard all the arguments from your side, and I still haven't changed my mind. I had to alter my position for the good of the company, but my feelings remain the same. They may accomplish miracles, but they're too sterile, too impersonal. I'm not ready to live in the year 2001."

They argued briskly throughout the excellent meal, each enjoying the quickness of the other's mind, the agile parry and thrust. York nabbed the last piece of garlic bread from under Tracy's nose and chewed it consideringly as he listened to her last argument. "Nope," he said finally as Martha withdrew their dishes. "I may have to live with them, but I don't have to like them."

They walked into the den with their coffee and sat

next to each other on the couch. "Anything else you don't like about this modern world?" Tracy asked, still amused by the unexpected burst of candor.

"Sure," he replied promptly with a level look. "Duty calling when I'm doing my damndest to make love to a particularly stubborn woman."

"What else?" She refused to back down or show discomfort.

"Stubborn women."

"What else?" she persevered, hoping he had exhausted the subject.

"Clothes, regardless of how fetching, when they cover what I would sell my soul to be gazing at." His eyes never left hers, but she felt as if she were being slowly and tantalizingly unwrapped.

"Has anyone ever told you that your mind runs on a single track?"

"Yes, but I don't think it was a complaint."

"Tell me about your father," she requested, conceding defeat.

"I inherited my tenacity and finesse from him." He grinned modestly.

"God help us," she murmured piously.

"He has greenhouses staggered all over his property at the Cape and breeds tuberous begonias."

"Don't you *grow* flowers?" she asked, perplexed.

"Most people do, but I'm convinced that his are doing illicit things in the dark because they're reproducing at an alarming rate."

"We were discussing your father," she reminded him, veering from what seemed to be his favorite subject. "Does he come to see you often?"

"He prefers that I visit him. Occasionally, when the Donovan stronghold is threatened, I call on him and he rallies around." He reached for her hand, lacing his fingers through hers, squeezing slightly. "Now it's your turn."

"To do what?"

"Tell me all about Tracy Maguire."

"What a glutton for punishment! I talked all the way home this afternoon. You heard about my parents, my brothers, my braces and my first car. What else is there?"

"You talked about the past. I'm interested in the future."

"Oh." There was a thoughtful silence before she warned, "It's going to sound pretty dull."

"I won't go to sleep on you," he promised.

"Well, my work is in the immediate future. There are so many things breaking in this field, it's a constant challenge."

"That's it?"

"I told you it wasn't exciting."

"What about your personal life?"

"Marriage, eventually, and a family. Combined with work, if possible."

"You're forgetting something," he reminded her, placing her hand on his thigh and covering it with his. "Where do I fit in?"

Her eyes slowly met his. "I don't think you do," she said bravely.

"The hell I don't. You're not walking away from me."

How did he manage to make such casually uttered words sound so threatening? she wondered. "York, I come from a long line of people who loved, married and remained faithful. I'm just not equipped to handle an affair."

He rose, pulling her up with him. "If we start discussing your equipment, I'll miss my plane. Get your things and I'll take you home."

"That's ridiculous. You still have to get ready. I'll take a cab."

"No way," he said tersely. "Get your purse."

"If it'll make you feel any better," she said, turning to the telephone, "I'll have him go the long way and you can pay for it."

York shot back his cuff, scowling impartially at his watch and Tracy.

"It'll be about ten minutes," she announced, hanging up. "Come on, I'll help you pack."

When the cabby arrived, sounding three short beeps of his horn, York's hand at her waist stopped her at the door.

She turned into his waiting arms. One long finger tilted her chin until her eyes met his. Her breath caught as she met the hungry flash of his eyes. His lips lowered to hers in a kiss that drew a soft moan from her throat and left her limp against him.

"Oh, God," he muttered against her lips, "I'm starved for the feel of you. I want your beautiful, naked body against mine, your softness flowing over me. I want—" He was interrupted by the beeping horn and muttered under his breath. His arms pulled her closer to his taut body. His lips pressed hers in a swift, hard kiss. "Remember this," he ordered. "When I get back, we'll pick up right here."

And now he was on his way back.

The day had passed quickly, as had all the others in his absence. Filled with minor emergencies, installing various bits of equipment, and supervising training classes, they had often stretched Tracy to her limit. She was grateful for the pace; it left her no time to think about York.

She did plenty of that, she reluctantly admitted to herself, at night. No matter how hard she drove herself, she lay awake, restlessly churning the bed into a mass of tangled covers. Erasing his memory was like trying to forget her own name. He had kept his promise. He had imprinted on her his taste, his smell, the feel of his strong, lean body. He had filled her with exquisite tension and, paradoxically, left her with an aching emptiness.

Now, as she drove through the evening traffic and turned on to the broad, maple-lined street leading to his house, she deliberately turned her thoughts from the evening ahead. York had accomplished what every man before him had failed to do. With his shock tactics, he had brought to life the dormant passion within her. Glancing into the rearview mirror, she grimaced at the shadows beneath her eyes. Her restless nights, she acknowledged to herself, were not the results of hard work. For the first time in her life, she wanted—no, needed—a man. And only York would do.

And why him? Why a single-minded, rude, perfectly *awful* man? She had absolutely no business falling in love with him. *Falling in love?* Her eyes strayed to some distant point as if the words had been written in space for her to study and memorize. Much against her will, she examined them. No, she promised herself firmly. Not love. Fascination maybe, possibly infatuation, but not love.

Who are you kidding? a silent, self-mocking voice that sounded remarkably like her own, inquired. You can lie to him and everyone else, but at least be honest with yourself.

Okay, she snarled silently. He's overbearing, presumptuous, imperious, sexy as hell, and I'm crazy about him.

But loving York Donovan, however it had happened, was a one-way street, she warned herself, a definite no-win situation. He wanted her as a bed partner—for as long as it took to complete her job, or until he tired of her—whichever occurred first. Marriage, or a long-term commitment, was not in his plan.

Forget about York's desires, she told herself. What

about hers? Where did he fit into her life-style, her plans? Nowhere, she admitted bleakly, after long moments of thought. True, she had no blueprint of her future, but somewhere in the years ahead were a husband and children. And from her they would receive the legacy of her parents—loyalty and constancy, a commitment to the family unit. She hoped it would be accompanied with the love and humor that graced her parents' lives.

Still wondering at a whimsical fate that had set her on a collision course with a man who wanted only an affair—one of many, if his reputation was to be believed—she parked her car next to his Mercedes. He answered the door bell as if he had been waiting with his hand on the knob.

"Hello, York." He looked leaner and darker, she thought, and more dangerous than ever.

He didn't answer. Instead his eyes dropped from her silky, long-sleeved creamy blouse to her well-fitting jeans and back up again. The next moment she was drawn inside, wrapped in his arms, and kissed with a hunger and strength that left her flushed and dazed. His hands brushed over her as if he were reassuring himself that she was as he remembered her.

"Hello, Tracy Maguire," he muttered, his breath warm against her face before he dropped one last hard kiss on her lips. The words were innocuous, but she sucked in her breath at the look on his face. Turning abruptly, he picked up her suede jacket, which had fallen to the floor, and hung it in the hall closet.

"Martha isn't here, but dinner's ready to put on the table," he said over his shoulder as he headed for the kitchen.

"What did she do, decide on the orphanage?" Tracy queried lightly. "Or did the hotel give her a better deal?"

"Neither," his answer was terse. "She's at a meeting."

Mentally shrugging her shoulders at his response, she carried a bubbling casserole into the dining room. He seated her in silence, a silence that persisted throughout the meal, becoming heavier with each forkful.

Deciding that someone had to say something, Tracy asked, "What took you to Australia?"

"Sheep."

"Sheep? As in lambs?"

"As in wool."

"Oh." Her voice remained cool, but her eyes betrayed her anger. He was in a foul mood and apparently had no intention of hiding it. She slanted another look at him and saw the lines of fatigue etched on his face. The fool! she thought with exasperation. He's dead on his feet and doesn't have the sense to go to bed.

Eventually they finished. Tracy could have been eating moldy bread and stagnant water for all she tasted. Swallowing had been difficult with York glaring at her as if she had long since overstayed her welcome.

Tired or not, the man was a boor, she thought, her temper overriding her normal survival instincts. "Have I done something wrong?" she finally asked in a cool little voice, indicating that she didn't give a damn one way or another.

"No." He watched with hard eyes as she slammed dishes on a tray and disappeared through the kitchen door. When she reappeared, his voice was silky. "Why do you ask?"

Normally, she would have caught the menace in his tone, the increasing aura of danger surrounding him as he slowly rose from his chair. Throwing caution to the wind, small fists planted on her hips, she said,

"Because you're in a rotten mood, and I'm tired of being your whipping boy. I feel about as welcome as a plague carrier. If you're mad, say so. If you got home hungry and tired, why didn't you have the good sense to eat and go to bed?"

He closed the distance between them with one lazy step. His voice was soft. "Are you through?"

She nodded once, her hair catching fire in the light and tumbling softly around her shoulders. "For now."

"You're here," he said with cool arrogance, "because I don't like to eat alone, and I'm damned tired of sleeping alone."

Tracy's eyes narrowed. "Just who the hell do you think you are?" Her shaken voice gathered momentum and volume. "And what do you think I am? Someone you call on the phone when you need to relieve your tension?" She whirled, heading for the front door. "I think your money, your position and your women have finally gone to your head, *Mr.* Donovan."

She turned to direct one final blast at him and was startled to find him right at her heels. Looking up, she caught a rueful grin on his face. It was the last straw. She pushed him hard, but York didn't budge. Instead, he grabbed her waist, hoisted her up and dumped her on the couch. He followed her down before she recovered from the first bounce.

"Let me go, you arrogant bastard!" Infuriated by his amusement, she twisted and squirmed, lashing out with her legs until they were clamped by his heavy thigh.

"Hold still, you little wildcat!" His voice was trembling with laughter. "I didn't mean it."

She fought until he had her secured hand and foot. His heavy body pinned her against the back of the couch and one large hand manacled her wrists above her head. Unable to move, she glared at him and swore. Using words that would have roused a long-shoreman to envy, she described his ancestry with ingenuity and eloquence.

"Mmmmff!" Her words ceased only when York's lips covered hers and remained there until her head rang with the need for air.

"My God, what a temper! Now calm down and listen to me." Tracy ignored his words as she concentrated on supplying air to her deprived lungs. "Your diagnosis was right," he conceded as she drew in a ragged breath. "But your prescription won't work."

His lips brushed her neck before he continued. "Hungry?" His laugh was short. "I'm starved—for you. And, yes, I'm tired. Tired of the games we've been playing, ending with you going off to your bed and leaving me to mine. For two weeks now, you've intruded on my business meetings and kept me from sleeping at night."

"I haven't been anywhere near you!"

"That's been the problem," he said grimly.

"We were stupid to think an arrangement like this would work." Her tone was an echo of his.

"Right!"

She twisted to see if he had slackened his hold. He hadn't. "It would probably be better for both of us if I left now."

"Wrong." His voice was husky as his lips drifted past the third button of her blouse, pulled open in the struggle, to the firm flesh above the line of her bra. "You manage to zero right in on the heart of the problem, but your solutions are a bit weak." She jerked in surprise as his eyes met hers in a hard, possessive glance.

Slowly he placed her palm against his chest. She could feel the thunder of his heart through the warm skin and soft, prickly hair. "Now, tell me that your heart isn't pounding to match mine, that the blood isn't roaring through your body like a freight train, that you don't want me as much as I want you, and I'll let you go."

"I can't," she whispered.

Her arms, which had been wedged, stiff with resistance, against his chest, slid to his shoulders, and she barely heard his sigh before his lips touched hers. The last of her tension dissipated at the curiously gentle, inquiring pressure. Her slim fingers slipped through his hair, dark now in the flickering light, shaping the proud head. Once again a fleeting image of the portrait presented itself. Had this man in her arms any of the poet, the dreamer in him, she wondered hazily. Or was he tempered steel, much as the broadsword held with such contemptuous ease by that ancient soldier?

York raised himself, leaning on one elbow, his green gaze sliding over her possessively. Tracy's hands rose to her breast, bare now but for a lacy froth of a bra, in the ageless, feminine gesture of instinctive modesty. Her lovely eyes were uncertain, shaded with desire.

"Shh, love," he soothed in a gentling tone. His large hands enfolded hers and replaced them on his shoulders. "I won't hurt you." The softly growled words were interspersed with fleeting touches of his lips as they ventured from her earlobe, grazed the delicate ridge of her collarbone, and settled with a sigh on the high, firm swell of her full breast.

Tracy made one last attempt. "York." The word was a strangled whisper.

"What, love?" he murmured absently. The dark pleasure in his eyes took her breath away, and she forgot what she had been going to say.

Shock jolted through her as his thumb etched her rib cage and his hand settled possessively on her

stomach. Her protest was swallowed by the firm lips
that covered the full softness of her own.

She was breathless when he finally raised his head.
"No, York. No more!" Striving for firmness, she was
unnerved to hear the words sound breathless and full
of feminine pleading.

"Oh, yes, Tracy," he mocked, his eyes feasting on
her flushed cheeks and tousled hair. "Much more!"
His hands cupped her breasts, stroking, caressing.

"Stop it," she muttered thickly as she tried to move
away, only to find herself trapped between the velvet
couch and the muscular, hair-prickling wall of his
chest. "I can't think when you do that."

His chuckle was a soft, deep growl. "That's the
general idea." She was drawn taut as a bowstring
against him, and his demanding fingers tightened in
her thick hair, raising her head to his seeking lips. The
kiss that followed was more than Tracy had bargained
for. His tongue probed and tasted the sweetness of
her mouth, while his hands caressed her to a state of
reeling acquiescence. This has got to stop! her sensible self admonished.

Just at that moment, as the unpleasant voice of
reality was rearing its head, York raised himself on
one elbow, pulling off his shirt. The cool air, fanned
by his movement, was like a dash of cold water. Her
eyes flew open.

"No, York. No more." This time her voice was
sharp, decisive.

Their ragged breathing was in counterpoint to the
airy music filling the room. The snap of the fire was
the only other sound.

Tracy forced herself to stillness, aware of York's
struggle. The mood had changed too quickly. She lay
quietly, hardly daring to breathe, as he loomed over
her, waiting for his control to reassert itself.

"Why?" he rasped, his voice tight with restraint.

She met his eyes and flinched at the flame in them. A warrior indeed, scenting victory, unwilling to acknowledge the signal to retreat.

"York," she said quietly, "I'm neither a tease, nor a tart. The whole thing got out of control; I couldn't stop it before this." She continued deliberately, bravely maintaining eye contact. "And for that, you have to accept a certain responsibility."

"Are you going to tell me you didn't enjoy it?" His breathing had steadied and his eyes were cooling to the familiar silver challenge.

"Not at all," she replied, disturbingly aware of the weight of his heavy thigh keeping her immobile. After a brief, internal battle, she admitted with her usual honesty, "I enjoyed it far too much for my peace of mind."

Keeping a wary eye on the man hovering over her, she prodded his chest with a pink-tipped finger. "You, Mr. York Donovan," she said, maintaining a cool, dry humor with difficulty, "are a dangerous man. I can see that keeping out of your bed is going to be far more difficult than I imagined."

He eyed her enigmatically for a long moment, then leaned down and with lingering sweetness kissed her. Ignoring her flushed cheeks, he got up and straightened his clothes.

Gentle hands closed on her shoulders and drew her back against a warm, solid wall of muscle. Her fingers fumbled with the pearl buttons on her blouse until his brushed them aside. Holding her breath, she stood immobile as his hands moved down the front of her blouse. He turned her to face him, brows drawn together in a heavy frown as he looked into her wide, strained eyes.

His lips brushed hers and she turned into his comforting embrace as if she were going home. Wrapping her arms around his waist, she rested her head on his broad chest. She didn't want to move, ever. She wanted to tell the world of her love for this very large, very gentle, extremely maddening man. But how could she tell the world when she couldn't even tell him. You don't bare your heart to a man who is sandwiching you between his last woman and the next.

He exhaled sharply, then stepped back, draped his arm around her shoulders and led her back to the couch. Grimacing at her apprehensive expression, he said, "Don't panic, this time we're going to talk." He settled her in the corner and moved to the next cushion.

Looking more composed than she felt, she thought about the last half hour and decided her resistance wasn't worth a plug nickel. And what about the rest of the evening, she worried, and tomorrow, and the days and nights following that? She had a feeling that York would not be wildly receptive to her objections, nor would he be willing to return to their former status. Triumphant warriors don't willingly retreat from a successful offensive position, she reminded herself grimly.

Trying to view the situation objectively—for all the good it would do when she confronted York—she acknowledged that it was not a viable one for her. She was not emotionally equipped to join the parade of women that ornamented York's life. When the time came, what she had to give was herself, not a commodity to be paid off in thousand dollar bills or diamonds. Surely, she thought crossly, since she had fallen in love so quickly, if she worked at it, she could fall back *out*.

The bitterness of his voice startled her. "Once, long ago, I made the mistake of marrying."

The words ringing in her ears like a death knell, Tracy stiffened. The rest was not going to be pleasant.

"I heard about your divorce," she said in a neutral tone.

"When I was well and truly secured, she didn't hesitate to inform me that my biggest attraction was my money." A wealth of anger and self-disgust lay beneath the cynical words.

"And you think all women are like that."

"Enough of them."

"So you never plan to marry again." Her tone matched the objective statement.

"Right. But that needn't affect us." Shifting his weight, he turned and captured her hand. "Honey, I've never wanted a woman the way I want you. Stay with me, live with me, and you can have anything you want."

"Except marriage." She removed her hand, rubbing her arms to chase away a sudden chill.

"That's not important," he said impatiently. "I'll take care of you in all the ways that a man cares for his woman."

"Sorry," she said, standing and smoothing her skirt over her hips. "I'm not for sale."

He got to his feet, towering over her, his green eyes cold. "Everyone has a price. Name it."

"We're right back where we started, aren't we?" she asked regretfully, reminding him of their first meeting.

"Oh, hell," he muttered, running a hand through his hair.

"I think we should just forget the whole thing. What happened earlier was a mistake, and it won't be repeated."

His retaliation was swift and to the point. "The hell it won't. You can no more stay out of my arms than I can yours," he stated grimly.

"You almost won the bet," she said bitterly. "You almost had me exactly where you said you would

. . . in your arms and in your bed. What more do you want from me?"

"Complete and total surrender."

He had to be joking! Stunned eyes lifted to his. "You're not serious."

"Believe me, honey, I've never been more so." There was no humor in his eyes now. "I didn't get where I am by being a loser. I fight by my own rules, I fight to the finish, and I win."

"But, surrender! You don't want a woman, you want a robot!"

"Wrong. I want you. And that automatically includes your stubbornness, your hot temper, your fascination with computers, as well as your vulnerability, your red hair, and your sexy little body. It simply means that in the end, you will admit that you belong to me heart, soul and body."

"You're stark raving mad! First you offer to buy me; then you say that only unconditional surrender will satisfy you. I don't think I like the stakes in this game at all." She retrieved her jacket from the closet, collected her purse and headed for the door. Turning back, she said, "Maybe, just so all the cards are on the table, I should explain that I have never yet slept with a man. But when I do, you can bet your megabucks it won't be with you!"

That the shuddering door remained on its hinges was a testament to the skill of an earlier generation of builders.

Chapter Seven

A brisk tap on the bedroom door and the aroma of coffee roused Tracy to a groggy state of consciousness the next morning. Her nose twitched as Meg placed a steaming mug on the bedside table.

"What did I do to deserve this?" she asked sleepily as she propped herself against a couple of pillows.

"Not a thing. I just decided that I had to get up before the birds if I wanted to see you."

"Is anything wrong?"

"Funny, that's exactly what I wanted to ask you."

"Oh." Blinking owlishly, she finally shook her head and said, "Let me wash my face and try to get my brain in gear. Don't go away, I'll be right back." She returned to find her aunt curled cozily at the foot of the bed sipping her coffee.

She crawled back beneath the covers and lifted her mug in an appreciative gesture. "Now I'm beginning to function. What's on your mind, stranger?"

"Plain and simple curiosity," Meg admitted shamelessly. "I know you're doing fine with the conversion, but how is the situation with York going?"

Tracy grimaced. "I think it would be fair to say that I almost lost the first major battle, but I intend to win the war."

"Oh, dear." Meg sighed. "Should I play the heavy aunt and bar the door?"

"No, you stay just as you are. I don't need a phalanx of relatives protecting me from the big, bad wolf."

"About this war . . . are you sure you want to win if it means walking away from York? After all, he's quite a man and . . . packaged very nicely," Meg murmured with a very feminine gleam in her eyes.

Tracy crossed her legs tailor fashion, resting her mug precariously on one knee. "It's funny," she mused. "When I left California, I had nothing on my mind but doing such a fantastic job out here that my boss's eyes would pop. Not a thought in the world that I would meet a man who would take my mind off computers and turn it to things like orange blossoms, cozy evenings at home and children. I had that neatly programmed for the future, to be available just at the right time."

"And?"

"And then a maddening, bullheaded man came along and upset my nice, neat plans. It took me a long time before I'd even admit that I wanted him quite desperately. But it won't work."

"I don't understand. He's presentable, has a wicked sense of humor, and certainly has enough money to keep the wolf from the door. What's the problem?"

"The problem is that he wants a playmate, and I'm just not the bunny type."

"Are you sure?"

"That I'm not a bunny?"

"Very funny! Are you so sure you know what he wants?"

"He made it very clear. A temporary arrangement is what he said, and that's exactly what he meant. He has a very cynical outlook on marriage."

"Sounds like someone really did a number on him."

"Well and truly," Tracy agreed wryly. "He's not about to try it again, and I can't settle for less."

Meg's voice was sympathetic. "So what are you going to do?"

"What I'm going to *try* to do is what I planned in the first place. Keep him at arm's length, work like the devil to finish this job, and run back to California before it's too late."

"Do you think it will work?"

"I don't know." Tracy swallowed convulsively and closed her eyes over sudden stinging tears. She absolutely would not cry! "He told me last night that he wanted nothing less from me than complete and total surrender." She looked at Meg with vulnerable eyes. "If I ever made that sort of commitment, I don't think I would survive when the time came to leave. Oh, physically, I would," she said, responding to Meg's concerned expression. "But not emotionally."

"And what would you get from him?" Meg asked, finally breaking the heavy silence.

"Him. Totally. For a while." She smiled crookedly, contemplating the bleak future. "It would almost be worth it. Almost."

The sudden purr of the telephone startled them. Tracy reached for it with the same caution she would use to handle a scorpion. Only one person would be calling at this hour. "Hello." She listened with mounting ire and hung up without another word.

Meg's face was alight with amusement. "What could he possibly come up with at six in the morning to put that look on your face?"

"With his own inimitable charm, he ordered me to pack a bathing suit and whatever else I'd need for a swim at his place after work. Then he hung up before I could say a word!" Tracy's voice quivered with temper.

"Cheer up," Meg consoled. "The way you swim, at least you'll be able to keep your distance in the pool!"

Muttering something about drowning being too good for him, Tracy threw back the covers and headed for the closet. She tossed a diagonally striped dress in brilliant fall colors on the bed and dug out her bathing suit and a terry wrap. As an afterthought, she added slacks and a violet tailored shirt for later that evening. She was ready to leave at almost her usual time.

The day began with a flurry of telephone calls. Tracy went down to accounting in response to a pathetic plea from one of the keypunchers. She unraveled the minor problem and grinned at the woman. "Cheer up, Sandra. Another day or so and you'll be through in here. Just remember to put your cards in the computer room at the end of the day. Can you imagine how pleased Mr. Degner would be if any of them were lost or damaged and you had to come back?"

Laughing as the other woman shuddered, she turned to leave and almost careened into the burly department head. As usual, he glowered at her. And as usual, she beamed a bright smile at him and thought, once again, that he would look more at home in a wrestling ring than sitting behind a desk.

She ran up the two flights of stairs to her office and worked in uninterrupted silence until Mary opened her door. "Just two quick announcements," she said, nodding in sympathy at the preoccupied look on Tracy's face. "One, don't forget the company dinner, and—"

"What dinner?"

"The one on Saturday."

"Wait a minute. I think I missed something along the way. What are you talking about?"

"Every year York gives a dinner for the major and minor wheels of the company. It's on Saturday, and you're invited."

"But I work for SynTel."

"Believe it or not, he knows that. You're invited as a guest."

"What's the other thing?" she asked, deciding to deal with the dinner at another time.

"If you trip over a fireman in the hallway, don't run for the nearest exit. They're here to examine the new alarm and protection system in the computer area. They decided to check the sprinklers in all the other departments while they were at it, so they'll be around for a couple of days."

"Anything else?" Tracy asked, her eyes straying to the program on her desk.

"No. You can get back to your Chinese puzzle. See you later." Mary closed the door quietly as she left.

At five thirty Tracy answered the telephone with an abstracted "Yes?"

"Tracy?" At York's deep-voiced query, she straightened her back and stretched. "Can you be ready to leave in a few minutes?"

"No," she said coolly, "I have a few things to finish before I go." He wouldn't have hesitated to say the same thing if the situation were reversed, she reminded herself bracingly. So why was she holding her breath and waiting for an explosion that would register on the upper edges of the Richter scale? "Why don't you go on and I'll be at your place in about an hour?"

After an interminable silence, he said abruptly, "All right, see you then." A quiet click, indicative of prodigious control, ended the conversation.

That thirty-second conversation had accomplished several things, she thought as she stared at the papers on her desk. First, she had made a mild declaration of independence. Second, York was indeed, at least for the moment, treating her as he would any other consultant. And third, she would be driving her own car. She could always get herself home if things got a little sticky.

With those encouraging thoughts, she briskly turned to the program that could have easily been taken care of the next day and gave it her undivided attention for the next thirty minutes.

It was almost dark when she pulled up in front of the large house. Martha greeted her with a smile. "York's in the pool already. I'll take you right up to change or he'll be waterlogged by the time you get there."

Chatting amiably, they walked upstairs and Tracy headed automatically for Jean's room. Martha touched her lightly on the arm. "No, this way." She opened the door to a large, masculine room. It was the master bedroom. York's room.

At Tracy's startled expression, Martha nodded to a door at the far end of the room. "That leads directly down to the pool. York thought you'd be more comfortable going that way than wandering through the house in your bathing suit."

Martha urged Tracy to put her case on the bed. "Don't bother with a towel. We keep a supply by the pool. Is there anything else you need?"

"No, thanks. I brought everything."

"I'll say good night then. Dinner is ready any time you want it." She looked mildly embarrassed for a second. "I'm going to a movie with some friends, and York said he would handle everything."

"No problem," Tracy assured her. "What are you going to see?"

"Love's Wicked Flame," Martha said with a twinkle that brightened her blue eyes. "But don't tell York. I'd never hear the end of it."

"You're a lady after my own heart," Tracy said, grinning as she opened her case. "Enjoy!"

Pulling off her dress with more haste than grace, she placed it and her neatly folded undergarments on a nearby chair. She stepped into her bathing suit, a black-and-white striped affair with high-cut legs and crossed back straps. She moved to a full-length mirror, then brushed her hair and clipped it at her nape with a heavy tortoise barrette. Her fingers fiddled nervously as her eyes took in the room reflected in the mirror.

She had the feeling there was more to her being in York's room than mere convenience. If it was another ploy to make his presence felt—it was working! The solid oak furniture and the massive bed behind her, covered with a forest green spread, might as well have had his name embossed in brass studs. The room was neat, fairly shouting with aggressive masculinity, and touched with the aroma of his expensive, spicy aftershave. She was overwhelmed with a sudden awareness of him.

Taking a moment to assess the room, she looked around appreciatively. The walls and floors were done in muted shades of green. A large floor-to-ceiling bookcase against one wall, containing an eclectic selection of books, proclaimed him a reader. But the bed dominated the room.

"I don't care if it's big enough for six," she muttered aloud. "He's going to be in it alone tonight!"

The stairway was well lighted, and when she emerged through the double doors at the bottom, she gasped in amazement. If she had given it any thought, she might have been prepared. No kidney-shaped pool squeezed in an extra few square yards was this!

Close to Olympic size, it was a pool for a serious swimmer. And it was enclosed in large, thick panes of glass that reached to a high, domed ceiling. During the day it would undoubtedly look out over the tree-covered acreage. At night, with the subtle lighting, it was a designer's dream. White wrought-iron furniture padded with brightly striped material, large potted trees and luxuriant ferns surrounded the pool.

The water erupted suddenly and York hefted himself easily over the side of the pool to stand in front of her. A sudden tension crackled between them as he examined her bathing suit, which faithfully followed the enticing curves of her body.

"What?" he asked in mock disappointment. "No skimpy bikini?"

"You said I was here to *swim*," she retorted, eyeing the pool with anticipation. It was either that or examine his long-legged body as hungrily as he was studying hers, and that would definitely lead to trouble. She could already feel an alarming increase in her pulse rate at his closeness. Her hands were clenched at her sides so they wouldn't stray to the thatch of wet, springy hair covering his broad chest.

"I'm dressed to do exactly that," she reminded him briskly. "Oh, I don't have a cap. Will my hair clog up the filter or anything?"

"No. You can even undo that thing," he said, pointing to the barrette, "if you want to."

"Thanks, but I don't like my hair in my face when I swim."

There was a long moment while they stood, just looking at each other, barely breathing. Tracy cleared her throat nervously. "Why are we just standing here?"

Without moving, York seemed to shake himself. "Damned if I know. Last one in gets dinner on the table!"

The two bodies hit the water as one. They swam lazily for a few minutes, York allowing her to set the pace. Suddenly Tracy tapped him on the shoulder, said, "You're it!" and shot away. York was right on her heels, following underwater to the deep end. For a while he was content to coordinate his moves with hers in a series of rolls and turns, surfacing for air, and then diving once again.

A playful thrust of Tracy's foot against his thigh ended the aquatic ballet. With a powerful lunge, he captured her ankle and hauled her into his arms. His long legs wrapped around hers, plastering her body to his, while his hands easily subdued her flailing arms. They rose slowly to the surface and Tracy's gasp for air was cut off as York covered her lips with his. When the kiss ended her fingers were tangled in his thick hair and his arms were pressing her body tightly against his. She leaned against him, waiting for her breathing to slow down and the strength to return to her limbs.

"Mmm, even chlorine smells good on you," he muttered, his mouth touching her earlobe.

Vaguely remembering how the whole thing had begun, Tracy sputtered, "You were supposed to *tag* me!"

"I just did," he explained with a boyish grin that was almost her undoing. "Probably the rules are different in the East," he continued solemnly.

He prodded her gently to the side and lifted himself to the deck in one fluid movement. Bending down, he grasped her beneath her arms, lifting her as he straightened.

"Are you game for a race?" he asked.

"How far?" she queried cautiously, her eyes gleaming with anticipation as she bent her head to check the clasp on the barrette.

"Five laps?"

"I think I need a handicap," she said decisively as her eyes measured him from his large feet to the top of his dark, wet head.

"Half a lap," he agreed as they walked to the far end.

"Loser does the dishes." She smiled innocently at him.

"Why do I have the feeling I'm being hustled?" he asked as she leaned forward, waiting for his signal. His eyes lit with appreciation as she exploded in a flat racing dive. His muscles tensed as she reached the halfway mark and he hit the water in a dive as expert as her own.

The next few minutes were ones of utter concentration for Tracy. Never had she appreciated her swimming coach so much as now. At each end, she dipped forward in a flip turn, paring seconds off her time as she pushed off the wall. By the last lap, she could feel York narrowing the gap between them. Her hand lunged forward to touch the end of the pool just as a large, tan one did the same.

They pulled themselves onto the deck and sat, regarding each other with a smile. "I'll show you my trophies," Tracy wheezed, "if you'll show me yours."

"Is that something like etchings?" he asked with interest as he reached out to squeeze water from her dripping ponytail.

"Except that my intentions are pure!"

"And mine aren't?"

"You said it, not me."

"Come on," he said, pulling her to her feet and directing her to the doors leading to his room. "Go on up and take a shower."

She looked at him uncertainly. "Should I use Jean's room?"

"No. Martha is having it redecorated. Use mine. I'll take one down here."

Thirty minutes later, she left the bathroom. Not only was it the size of a large bedroom, it had a hot tub, sprawling ferns that seemed to thrive in the moist heat, and a large shower that unexpectedly shot out jets of water from various sources. It had taken considerable discipline simply to shower, dry her hair, and leave.

Her thigh-length wrap was of fine terry cloth, classically styled like a man's long-sleeved shirt. She carelessly secured the lower three buttons and reached up to free her hair from beneath the collar as she entered the bedroom. The movement of her arms created a navel-deep opening in the robe and revealed an intriguing glimpse of soft curves.

"My God," York's voice rasped from the other end of the room. "An artist would sacrifice his hope of salvation if he could paint you like that!"

Tracy froze, her breath locked somewhere deep in her lungs as she spotted him leaning against the door.

York walked out of the shadows, a towel carelessly knotted at his hips. His gaze slid over her, potent as a caress. She could feel the warmth of his eyes as they touched her fiery hair and drifted down to the plunging V of the stark white robe that covered her gold-toned body. His voice was husky as he touched her face. "A man could live on your beauty and light for the rest of his life," he murmured, smoothing his thumbs along the slant of her wide, gold-flecked eyes.

His fingers threaded in her hair, lifting her face to his. "You're a potent combination, Red. The beckoning of a woman; the retreat of an innocent." His grin was a wry twist of his well-shaped lips. "It makes a man want to protect and, at the same time, ravish you."

This wasn't going at all according to plan, she thought dazedly. She was supposed to be well protected by slacks and a blouse when next they met, not three buttons away from nakedness.

"York," she whispered, and as had happened so many times before, her parted lips drew his like a magnet and her words were lost. One kiss, she thought, when she was able once again to think coherently. That's all it takes. One kiss and my very blood and bones cry out for this man. Her hands kneaded the corded strength of his shoulders and lingeringly smoothed the hard muscles of his back.

"Tell me you want me," he demanded huskily. "Tell me that you can't sleep at night because I'm not there beside you, that you toss and turn in the darkness the way I do." The words were punctuated with small, nipping kisses on her eyelids, her temple, cheekbones, and earlobes until she was on fire.

He raised his mouth a whisper away, his warm breath on her lips. "Tell me that you need me as much as I need you. That your body aches the way mine does. This time, I need the words, Red. It's not enough that your hands touch me with a hunger that matches my own." He shook her lightly, bringing her eyes up to meet the green blaze of his.

He lowered her hands to her sides and moved away a fraction of an inch, so that while she still felt the heat of his body, he was no longer touching her. "I have to know how you feel." His soft words were a command. *"Now."* His body was tense, guarded, as he watched her eyes darken with emotion.

"I . . ." Rejecting the word she yearned to say, she settled instead for what he asked to hear. "I need and want you," she whispered, her breathing fast, shallow. The blaze of triumph in his eyes gave her the courage to finish. "But I told you before, I can't live like that."

"Idiot," he whispered. "I'm not asking you to tack

on a scarlet letter for the world to see. Stay with me. Let me love you, take care of you, show you just how it can be with us.

"Say yes," he ordered with a self-mocking smile.

She looked up with eyes clouded by desire and saw the request reflected in the taut lines of his face, the throb at his temple, and in the tremor running through his strong arms.

"Tracy?"

She was aware that the flame he had ignited earlier had not been extinguished. It had merely been banked, waiting for a spark to flash and consume her. But the memory served another purpose. It reminded her of the bleak space between them. She shook her head slowly from side to side.

He stepped back. "I think you'd better get dressed," he said tautly. *"Now,"* he snapped, as she hesitated. "If you want to make it through that door."

Alerted by the warning in his voice, his taut stance, she had a fleeting vision of a fur-clad Celt tossing a protesting woman over his shoulder and striding down a grassy path into the darkness. She took one last look at his hard face, grabbed her clothes, and fled into the bathroom.

Fifteen minutes later, as she was bracing herself for the next confrontation, York knocked on the door and walked in. "Are you hungry?"

"For what?" she asked suspiciously.

"Food, woman, food! I'm so hungry I could eat the hooves of a rhinoceros."

Relieved, Tracy linked her elbow with his and looked up at him with laughing eyes. "You have very peculiar tastes, Mr. Donovan. I suppose it's not a fatal character flaw, but I thought I should mention it." Her stomach rumbled, ruining the effect of her prim little lecture.

His deep laughter blended with her chuckle as he lifted her in his arms and carried her downstairs.

"I do have legs, you know," she informed him.

"Very pretty ones, too," he agreed. "I might even go so far as to say gorgeous."

"I'm trying to tell you that I can walk as well as the next person."

"Don't spoil my fun," he commanded. "I like carrying a gorgeous woman in my arms."

"Do you do it often?" she asked sedately.

"Not nearly as often as I'd like to," he grumbled.

As they ate, Tracy commented on his beautifully decorated bathroom, admitting she had never been in a hot tub. "I'm going to have to get one of those little jewels."

"You can share mine," York offered.

"I meant, when I go home."

"As I said," York's voice lost its bantering tone, "you can share mine."

"Very generous of you," Tracy commented lightly as she poured coffee in their cups, "but with air fare the way it is, it would be cheaper to buy my own." She changed the subject smoothly. "Do you want a piece of this luscious apple pie that Martha left?"

After dinner, York reached in the pocket of his jeans, mumbled something and felt the other pockets.

"What's the matter? Did you lose something?"

"No. I forgot it. Be back in a minute."

Tracy was still staring at the door in surprise when he reappeared. "Come here," he said, tugging at her hand. He led her into the hallway, stopping in front of a gold-framed oval mirror. "Close your eyes, and keep them closed."

He muttered as he fumbled with something, and she had a sinking feeling that she knew what was coming. The feeling became a certainty as his fingers ruffled her hair, then lingered at her earlobes and neck.

"Now!"

York's eyes blazed with possessive satisfaction. The earrings and necklace reminded her of a shimmering waterfall. The cascade at her ears shone through her tousled, flaming hair. The larger one fell between her breasts.

York reached around her, released several buttons of the violet shirt and pulled the fabric to the tips of her shoulders, creating a deep V neckline.

The jewelry blazed even in the muted light of the hallway. The effect was dazzling, electric. It made her beautiful, she thought in wonder, not realizing that it merely enhanced her vibrant, lovely face.

York seemed content to remain there, absorbing, almost devouring, her. Tracy touched with a slim finger first the necklace, then each earring.

"How beautiful. They're diamonds, aren't they?" she asked in wonder.

"Of course." His tone was indulgent.

Nodding slowly, thoughtfully, she turned away from the mirror and, incidentally, out of his arms. His tone, as much as the jewelry itself, disturbed her. How often had this scene taken place, with how many other women; if not in front of this mirror, then another one?

Chapter Eight

Walking into the den, aware that he was right on her heels, she poured herself a glass of wine. "They really are beautiful," she repeated, deliberately seating herself in a wing chair. A large occasional table stood between it and the couch where York reluctantly sat.

"You haven't said thank you," he reminded her idly. She was dismayed at the stubborn set of his jaw and the growing look of determination in his eyes.

"I thank you for the thought," she said finally. "But not for the gift," she continued steadily in the ominous silence, "because I can't accept them." Sighing inwardly, she watched his eyes silver in anger.

His quiet question surprised her. "Why not?"

"They're too expensive!" she blurted without thinking.

"Do you have any idea how much money I have?"

"No. And I don't want to know!"

"I have so much," he persisted, "that it would be an insult if I gave you something inexpensive."

"But I don't want you to buy me anything! Take me out to dinner, bring me flowers, take me to a play, but don't do things like this." She touched the necklace.

"Why not?" he asked again.

Her troubled sigh matched the look on her face. "York, we're in different leagues. I don't belong here. Why don't you go find some oil heiress to play with? Or a movie star, or anyone who understands the crazy rules of the game we're playing." Her voice had become sharp with frustration.

"Why not?" he demanded again, his eyes pinning her to the chair.

Deliberately, she studied his hard face. Her voice was even when she finally spoke. "There are several names for women who give themselves to men in exchange for expensive gifts. I don't like any of them."

She cringed inwardly at the look of fury on his face. "By God, I don't think of you like that, and I won't have you doing it!"

"I didn't until you wrapped me up in these." Once again her hand drifted up to touch the necklace.

"Then take the damn things off!" His voice was as savage as his eyes.

She fumbled with the clasp, sudden tears blurring her sight. She ducked her head, grateful when her unruly hair fell forward, covering her cheeks. "I can't get it off," she sniffed.

"Are you crying?" he asked in amazement.

"No," she wept, her voice cracking.

She was swept up, bundled against his chest and lowered as he returned to his seat on the sofa, holding her firmly in his lap. "So you're not crying?" he asked, humor warming his voice.

"Of course not," she maintained as a tear fell on his shirt.

"Well, in that case, hold your hair up while I figure out how to open this clasp."

She pulled her hair forward, carefully averting her face as he fiddled with the catch.

"There!" He plucked the necklace off and carelessly tossed it on the table.

"I can do the earrings," she said quickly as he slid his fingers into her hair. She squirmed, trying to slide off his lap, but a strong arm around her middle held her in place. She dropped the earrings in his cupped hand and he quietly placed them on the table. Rebuttoning her shirt, she sat turned away from him, her back stiff.

"Look at me, Tracy." It was quiet, but nonetheless a command.

She shook her head, feeling foolish, wishing the embarrassing situation was over and wondering how to end it. She didn't have long to think about it.

York suddenly tilted her back so she was lying across his lap, her head supported in the crook of one strong arm. "Better now?" he asked, his eyes searching her face.

She nodded. "I wish you could understand," she said, knowing that he didn't, even though he was willing to indulge her for the moment.

"I wish I could, too," he replied. "I don't know how many women I've given—" He stopped on a strangled note, as if he had suddenly received a karate chop to the larynx.

"Exactly," Tracy said with asperity. "Come on," she said, freeing herself from his suddenly lax arms. "Let's clean the kitchen before Martha gets back." He followed along, damning himself for a fool with every step, but knowing that she needed the flurry of activity to regain her equilibrium.

At the end of the few minutes it took to return the room to its typically pristine condition, Tracy conceded that he wielded a mean dishtowel. As she placed the last dish on the shelf York slipped his arm around her waist and guided her back to the den.

They sat in silence, a more comfortable one this time, enjoying the evening cricketsong through the open window.

"What are you thinking about?" he inquired lazily.

"Nothing. Everything. How nice it is not to be fighting with you."

"It will be like this every day."

"When?" Her voice was husky and her lowered lids hid the wild hope that suddenly filled her.

"When you move in with me."

Her body stilled as the hope died. Fool! You *knew* that was all he wanted, she reminded herself disgustedly. All he would offer. Why set yourself up for such a letdown? Right from the beginning, his intentions were clear, remember? Despite the stern lecture, the pain remained.

She glanced at her watch. "York, it's getting late. I've got to go."

"It's early yet."

"Not by my standards. I'd better collect my clothes." She went upstairs, knowing from the stubborn set of his jaw that she had not heard the last on the subject of her moving in. And she needed time to marshal her arguments.

"What?" she asked, realizing that York had been talking as he followed her up the stairs.

"I said I could have a moving van pick up your things at Meg's and you could be settled in by tomorrow night."

"No, I don't think so," she disagreed lightly, closing her case and checking to see that she had left nothing behind.

He scowled as she picked up the case. "What do you mean, you don't think so?"

"Just what I said." Her voice was cool. She had used those few precious moments to deliver another pointed lecture to herself. Whatever happened during the next few minutes, she promised herself, she would not give in.

"It wouldn't work. It might be great for you, but I would be uncomfortable. Therefore, it wouldn't work." She looked at him with a raised brow, ignoring his frown, and pointedly checked her watch.

He was leaning against the door when she turned. She took a deep breath, flinching inwardly at the dark look on his face, knowing she wouldn't be able to leave the room unless he chose to let her.

"York," she said, selecting her words carefully, preferring to avoid a confrontation until she was in a less vulnerable position, "can't we talk about this when we have more time?"

"You said you'd be uncomfortable. I want to know why." Faced with her stubborn silence, he persisted. "If we're speaking of comfort, this house is more luxurious than Meg's. I'd see to it that you had everything you needed or wanted."

Deliberately she studied the angry man before her, knowing that he was going to get angrier.

"The first day we met, I told you that you couldn't afford me," she reminded him evenly. "Now, apparently, I'll have to add, you can't give me what I need."

"What the hell are you talking about?" he snarled.

"For a clever man, you certainly need to have things spelled out for you. To put it very simply, I would be unhappy in such an arrangement for the same reason I won't accept your jewelry." Her head lifted proudly, even though she was quaking at the fury in his face. "I am nobody's kept woman."

He straightened slowly and moved toward her. "Is that what you feel like in my arms? A *kept woman?*"

She eyed him nervously, wondering if he planned to throttle her now or wait until she maddened him further.

"Well?" he prodded, his silver eyes demanding as his voice whip-cracked over her head.

"No," she admitted quietly. "I only feel that way when you try to buy me."

The silence was unnerving. She darted a look at him to find him staring at her with a strange look in his eyes. "Exactly what is it you want from me?" he asked. "What more can you want than what we already have? And have any time we get within ten feet of each other?"

"York," she said, trying to inject a note of humorous complaint in her voice, "I'm not really at my best this late at night. Couldn't we continue this downstairs over a cup of coffee?" Her mind was calculating the distance between the kitchen and the front door rather than the benefits of a hot drink.

"Not until you answer my question," he said, lounging once more against the door. "What do you want that I can't give you?"

"I told you before, our life-styles are different. The day in your office when we made our crazy agreement, I was intrigued, challenged and"—her eyes met his steadily—"so very cocky. I didn't think you had a chance." She drew in a long, shuddering breath. "I don't think I have ever underestimated an opponent so badly."

She raised a hand as he started to speak. "Let me finish. I want more than just a few weeks in your bed. You've taught me a lot about myself, about being a woman." Her smile twisted, despite her resolution. "You've got me so tied up in knots, I don't know which way is up. But if I end it here and now, I'll survive. And in time, maybe I can find another man—"

"Like hell you will!"

"—who can make me feel the way you do," she persevered, ignoring his snarled statement. "And who will offer me permanence and fidelity."

"And what about money?"

"I thought I showed you that money wasn't important to me."

"It's easy to turn down a trinket if you think you can get your pretty little hands on the whole bank account." It took a moment for the quiet cynicism of his words to penetrate.

Tracy's eyes, after a moment's stunned incomprehension, became frozen flecks of green and gold. "I don't deserve that," she said with numbed calmness. Wrapped up in her own misery, she was heedless of the look of agonized regret that registered momentarily on York's face. "Get out of my way, York." The look on her face suggested that she would walk over or through him, if she had to. He moved.

By the time she reached the front door, her cold misery had become rage. She was determined, however, to leave on a note of dignity. The fact that York had somehow beat her to the door and was once again blocking her way weakened her resolve a bit. His next words blew it to smithereens.

"All right," he said abruptly, as if he were laying down the law at a board meeting. "You want permanence, you'll get it." His hard face was closed, concealing his emotions. "I'll marry you, as soon as the law allows. I'll call my lawyers in the morning—"

"You'll *what?*" she said incredulously. "*Marry* me? Listen to me, you big-headed, arrogant oaf; *watch my lips*. I wouldn't have you if you served yourself up on a silver platter with an apple in your mouth! And you could probably even do that! With all your money, you could have a tray custom made, and for all I know, you even own a damned apple orchard!"

Her temper was not assuaged a whit by the grin he was unsuccessfully trying to control, even as he eyed her warily. Nor did the quiver in his voice help as he said, "Calm down, honey. I—"

"I don't know what makes you think women are standing in line waiting to marry you," she rolled on. "Oh, yes, how could I forget? It's all those hotels and oil wells and stores and plants, and for all I know, cranberry bogs and codfish oil! Well, you call your lawyer, now, call a whole cordon of them! But you'd better find yourself another woman, because I wouldn't touch any of it, or you, with a bargepole!"

"Now, just a damn minute!" His humor was gone in an instant, and Tracy stared into silver eyes blazing with anger. "I didn't mean—"

"You can't know how you relieve my mind," she assured him, taking advantage of his shift in position to open the door. "And you can tell your legal crew I won't even sue you for breach of promise!" And on that note, she swung out, slamming the door with a mirror-shifting, crystal-tinkling thud.

Martha walked in through the still shuddering door. Her mouth opened and snapped shut without a word at the look of fury on York's face.

They both flinched as a car door slammed.

The days that followed, contrary to all the laws of nature, both dragged and flew by. York, so Mary told Tracy, was tied up with a merger that had developed a snag. Either that was true, or he had a well developed sense of preservation, because he was conspicuous by his absence from her office.

His temper, though, was just as unpredictable as hers. Mary complained humorously that it was like working between two caged tigers, complete with lashing tails and extended claws. Other unfortunate souls who had to deal with the combatants heaved sighs of relief when they escaped with their skins intact.

Another source of irritation to Tracy was the bustle and excitement whenever the conversation turned to the forthcoming company dinner.

"What are you going to wear?" Mary asked one day as they were eating lunch in the cafeteria.

"I'm not going." Tracy concentrated on her salad, trying to ignore Mary's stunned silence.

"I think you should reconsider," she said finally. "I've been involved in the seating arrangements, and you, Meg and York's father are all placed at the head table."

"Tough," Tracy said succinctly.

But much against her will, Tracy was feeling a bit like a fly entrapped in the proverbial spider's web. She was aware of details falling into place around her. Several days before, Meg had waved an engraved invitation at her as soon as she walked in the door.

"Look! From York. Wasn't he nice to include me in this shindig?" She tossed another one to Tracy with a casual, "Here's yours. York called this afternoon apologizing for not sending them sooner. He also explained that he would be at a late meeting the night of the dinner and has asked his father to call for us."

"I don't want to go," she said now, repeating to Mary what she had told Meg. "York Donovan is a pain in the neck, and I don't want anything to do with him or his dinner!"

"Unfortunately, you're not in a position to satisfy your personal whims," Mary reminded her. "Your conversion is touching every department in this building. If you're not there to represent SynTel, there'll be hell to pay, and I have a feeling it will come from several different directions."

As if to confirm Mary's prediction, the telephone in Tracy's office rang two hours later. Grimacing, she recognized the plummy voice of SynTel's president. "Tracy, dear girl, I'm just calling to find out how you are . . . and, incidentally, to see how your schedule is holding up."

"I'm fine, Mr. Sanders," she acknowledged cautiously, waiting for the shoe to fall. He was not a man who called his far-flung reps with words of encouragement. "And the schedule is even better. We're actually ahead in some of the departments."

His voice was just the right blend of hearty approval and complacency. "Good, good! I knew from the start you were the right one to send out there." He grew even more expansive. "I understand you're representing us at Donovan's annual company dinner. He rarely invites outsiders, so it's quite an honor, my dear, an honor indeed. I know you'll do us proud."

Tracy glared at the telephone once the connection was broken and she had slammed down the receiver. She detected York Donovan's fine hand in that call. Too bad they weren't speaking. She had a few choice words she wanted to share with him.

She picked up the phone once again and dialed a number on the intercom. "Mary? Just how formal is this thing?"

"Very," Mary said dryly. "All the stops are pulled out. Imagine the Academy Awards and go from there."

"Thanks. You've just made my day."

"I take it you'll be there?"

"Yes. I changed my mind. You don't sound surprised, though."

"I just put a call through to you from California, remember? SynTel's owner, I believe."

"You wouldn't have any ideas about what prompted that call, would you?"

"It might have had something to do with the complimentary invitation he received, along with a letter explaining that you were being asked to represent your company," Mary admitted with amusement, and laughed outright at the infuriated muttering coming through the receiver.

If ever a celestial representative had been assigned to watch over a certain redheaded computer specialist, he was obviously not attending to business, Tracy decided glumly as she left work Friday.

Meg pounced on her before she even had time to close the door. "Tracy! Good, you're home at a decent hour for once. Don't sit down; we've got to go."

"Go where?" she asked with a sinking feeling.

"Shopping. And we only have a few hours left until closing time."

"For what, as if I didn't know?"

"Don't play dumb. I've been through your closet, and you don't have a thing that will do for tomorrow night." Ignoring the obstinate look on Tracy's face, Meg continued rapidly, "And neither do I. Oh, Tracy, it's so exciting! I haven't been to something this glamorous for a long time, and I want us to look our best. Please come. At least to help me find something."

Tracy had never been able to resist her favorite aunt, and this was no exception. Within minutes they were in the car, and Meg was backing out of the driveway. "Do we have to go into Boston?" Tracy asked, dreading the evening traffic.

"No way," Meg said blithely. "I have some favorite boutiques here in the suburbs. They're expensive, but what they carry is worth the extra money. You'll see."

After the third shop, they were getting desperate.

"Come on," Meg said grimly, looking at her watch. "We've just got time to get to Marci's. She'll have something for us."

"Then why didn't we start out there?" Tracy asked reasonably.

"Because, although she's a good friend, she charges the very earth, and I can't resist trying the other places first."

"Marci," Meg's voice was breathless as they entered the shop some twenty minutes later. "You've got to save us!"

A cool, tall blonde, impeccably dressed in black, looked up with a slight smile. "What's the matter, Meg? You look like a distraught Cinderella searching for a ballgown."

"Funny you should say that." Meg explained the situation, aware that time was marching on in its usual inexorable fashion.

Tracy could almost see Marci ticking off a mental inventory of her stock. "You want to wow them?"

Meg nodded. "We want to knock their socks off!"

"Okay, but it's going to cost you."

"Doesn't it always?" she asked humorously.

Marci briskly locked the door, dimmed the lights and ushered them into a large back room. "It's almost closing time," she said in response to Tracy's look of inquiry. Then she grinned impishly, ruining her cool image. "I don't often get a chance to take advantage of Meg, and I don't want to be interrupted."

She assessed them briefly in a businesslike way and ordered, "Okay, gals, strip down to the essentials while I go find something sexy and elegant."

Against her will, Tracy found herself caught up in the pleasurable anticipation of trying on lovely clothes. And Marci knew her business. Within minutes she had Meg clad in a gown that had them gasping.

"I knew it," Marci said in satisfaction. "I thought of you when it came in." The dress was pale green, just the color of Meg's eyes, and it brightened her red hair to almost the vibrant tone of Tracy's. It was a rustling taffeta with a fluted, pleated ruffle made to slide on or off the shoulders. Sashed at the waist, it fell to the floor in a graceful, full skirt.

Marci arranged the ruffle so it barely reached Meg's collarbone, leaving her shoulders and neck bare. "Wear your hair up, and don't you dare clutter up that neckline with jewelry. Drop earrings will be all you need."

"Now, you," she turned to Tracy. "Off with your bra." She eyed Tracy's firm figure, nodded decisively and said, "Yes, you can get away with it." She disappeared for a moment, calling out as she returned, "Close your eyes. If this does what I think it will, I want you to get the full effect."

Tracy did as she was bid, dutifully raising her arms and turning as Marci directed. The dress slithered softly down her body, and she heard Meg draw in a sharp breath.

"Even better than I thought," Marci exulted. "Take a look."

Tracy couldn't believe what she saw in the mirror. The dress was a shimmering black sheath softly clinging to her curves and slit on one side to mid-thigh. It was gathered high on one shoulder, leaving the other one bare.

"Walk over here," Marci commanded. The fabric gleamed with soft fire at each movement. "Turn around. Yes. That's it. Earrings and a bracelet. No more. Do you have the proper accessories?"

Later, substantially poorer but considering every penny well spent, the two women returned home. Settling down with a pot of tea between them, they propped their feet on the coffee table.

"Well," Meg said, pleasurably wiggling her toes, "now that you have the ammunition, what's the battle plan for tomorrow night?"

"I think," Tracy replied slowly, "it will be one of evasive action—carried off with discretion and élan, of course!"

"Of course!"

"He wants a representative of SynTel, and that's exactly what he'll get. I'll greet him and then make myself scarce. Too bad Jon won't be there," she mused. "Maybe I'll cultivate the new operations manager. He's a nice man."

"How dull," Meg commiserated.

"Not at all," Tracy maintained stoutly. "Believe me, *nice* will be a pleasant change after all the insults and high-handed treatment I've been dealing with lately."

"You know," Meg said shrewdly, "I have a feeling that this whole thing isn't going any too smoothly for York, either."

"How so?"

"I don't think he knows what's hit him. I doubt if he really loved his wife. It sounds like his reaction to what she did is more damaged pride and anger than anything else. And as for the parade that's followed ever since," she continued, gathering steam as she went along, "I think it was just a case of buying whatever was on the market!"

"You have such a charming way of putting things."

"I'll bet he never cared if the current woman in his life was blond, brunette, or redhead, as long as she was there when he wanted her."

Tracy stirred restively. "Mary said much the same thing. But I still don't see what that has to do with me."

"Good Lord, girl, wake up! The man never takes his eyes off you. And he has the devil's own time keeping his hands off you. I have the feeling he's just one step away from throwing you over his shoulder and locking you up somewhere."

"Come on, Meg!" Tracy felt a flush rising in her cheeks as she recalled his embarrassingly steady regard and an occasional feeling of having narrowly escaped some violent action.

"I think," Meg said deliberately, "that he never cared enough for any woman to be jealous, and it never mattered if one left because there were always others waiting in the wings."

"And I'm different?" Tracy asked cynically.

"You are! From where I'm standing, or sitting," she amended, acknowledging her comfortable position with a smile, "it doesn't look as though he's ready to turn you in for a newer model. Frankly, I think you've become a colossal headache for poor Mr. Donovan."

"Good! He deserves one!" Her satisfaction turned to curiosity. "Why do you say that?"

"Because he doesn't want to let you go, and the only way he can keep you is to change his entire life-style. After all," Meg said reasonably, "you've upset his nice and tidy life just as much as he has yours. I imagine he's doing some pretty heavy thinking right now."

"And what do I do in the meantime?"

"To bring him around to your way of thinking? Just what you've planned for tomorrow. Look gorgeous, be friendly but aloof and don't give up!"

Their eyes met in a purely feminine look, and they solemnly raised their cups in a toast. "To a successful campaign!"

She should have known it wouldn't work! Tracy seethed silently the following evening as she stood with York's long arm unobtrusively clamping her to his left side as they greeted his guests.

Two hours earlier, Meg and Tracy had descended the stairs to wait for York's father. They had placed their wraps and purses on a chair and examined each other one last time.

"We've done it," Meg stated positively.

"We'll knock 'em dead," Tracy agreed, nodding judiciously just as the door bell rang.

"I'll get it." Meg walked into the hall.

"Mrs. Forrest?" a deep voice inquired. There was a long silence, then a soft mumble of voices. Tracy turned at the sound of solid footsteps and the rustle of Meg's dress. Her mouth fell open at the sight of the man towering over her aunt. My heavens, was her first thought, they're cloning the Donovans!

An inch or two shorter than his son, he looked as though he played handball every day and ran marathons on the side. Why had she pictured him as an old man, happily tending a small garden and benevolently patting children on the head? she wondered. With his auburn hair touched lightly with gray and pure green eyes, he exuded the solidity of a giant redwood and the benevolence of a shark.

At the moment his gaze was directed at Meg with the total concentration of a man who has solved a puzzle of long standing. And Meg, Tracy noted with both empathy and amusement, was definitely rattled. Enjoying the sight of her usually imperturbable aunt flustered, Tracy waited quietly with a slight smile on her face.

"Tracy!" Meg dithered as if she had just remembered her niece's name. "This is, uh, Mr. Donovan. He . . ." Her voice faded away as if she had forgotten what he had done, was going to do or what she had intended to say in the first place.

He stepped around Meg, shifting his intent gaze to Tracy as he approached her. His green eyes deepened with appreciation as he encompassed her radiant beauty in one quick glance. "Now I begin to understand," he murmured obscurely with a hint of a grin. "Not Mr. Donovan, please," he requested, raising Tracy's outheld hand gallantly to his lips. "Marcus."

"Marcus," she agreed with a smile. This one was dangerous, but at least his lethal power was not directed at her. "My aunt's friends call her Meg," she added straightfaced.

"Is that a nickname?" he asked, turning back to Meg, his eyes lingering on the picture she made standing in the doorway.

"For Meghan," she replied faintly.

"Meghan." He tasted the word, seeming to savor it. "Yes, of course. Meghan."

And that seemed to settle that, Tracy thought. "Would you like a drink before we leave, Marcus?" she asked, as Meg had not yet found her voice.

"No, thank you." He withdrew his gaze from Meg's face long enough to glance at his watch. "Aside from the fact that I promised York to arrive early, I'm anxious to make an entrance with two such lovely ladies."

They arrived to find York standing in the center of the glittering ballroom, looking at his watch impatiently. Tracy swallowed dryly. She had never seen him in formal evening clothes. Standing out starkly against the pale walls, the luxurious fall of gold drapes and sparkling crystal chandeliers, he was magnificent. His eyes locked on her as she walked forward with Marcus and Meg. She struggled to remain cool under the proprietary gaze.

"Right on time," Marcus proclaimed, breaking the sudden tension between them. "Just as I promised."

"Meg, you are lovely," York said, kissing her lightly on the cheek. He clapped his father briefly on the shoulder. "Thanks." Their exchanged look was one of mutual satisfaction.

Turning to Tracy, he snagged her hand and moved away. "You're absolutely breathtaking tonight, but I'll tell you more about that later. Right now, I need you for something."

"Where are we going?" she protested as he pulled her along behind him, weaving a path through the tables to the entrance, where a large group had gathered.

"Didn't anyone tell you?" he asked in mock-surprise. "You're my hostess tonight. We're going to greet our guests."

Digging her nails into his hand, she balked. "Over my dead body! I'm not going to do it."

Halting so suddenly that she bumped into him, he smiled down at her with a daredevil gleam in his eyes. "If you get stubborn about this," he said calmly, "I'll do what I wanted to do the instant you walked in here on my father's arm."

"What's that?" she asked warily.

"Kiss you until you're breathless and begging for more."

"I don't believe you," she said boldly, pulling at her hand. "You wouldn't do that in front of all these people."

He laughed softly beneath his breath. "You still don't know me very well, do you?" He tightened his grasp, his intention written clearly on his face.

"No!" she said, capitulating in sudden panic. "I'll do it. But I'll get you for this," she muttered as he led her to the door, "if it's the last thing I do."

"I'm counting on it," he said blandly as he smiled at the first couple.

They greeted hundreds of people, then sat at the head table with Meg and Marcus and a sprinkling of board members and spouses. York briefly welcomed everyone and encouraged them to enjoy the evening.

He released her hand only while they ate dinner and promptly reclaimed it to begin the dancing. Later, when an enterprising and courageous young man asked Tracy to dance, York calmly pulled her closer and said shortly, "Sorry, not tonight."

They circulated, drifting from one table to another, Tracy's hand placed securely in the crook of York's arm. His only acknowledgement of its presence was the instant tightening of his muscles if she wriggled her fingers or attempted to remove them. She had no idea what she said. She remembered smiling a lot. And nodding. A lot.

As they returned to their table, a roll of drums gradually silenced the room. Now what? she wondered as York rose to face the curious and expectant crowd. She heard the rumble of his voice, but was distracted as she looked across the table. Meg, her cheeks flushed, was fiddling with her wineglass. She flicked an angry glance up at Marcus, whose eyes were fixed on her face, a slight curve to his firm lips.

Clearly at the end of her tether, Meg muttered, "Will you, for heaven's sake, *please* quit staring at me!"

He leaned forward and touched the stiff ruffle directly above her breast, smiling broadly as she jumped. "No," he said simply. "I haven't seen anything so lovely in years, and I can't take my eyes off you."

Tracy lowered her lashes to conceal the amusement in her eyes and thought how good Marcus and Meg looked together. Her attention returned abruptly to York when she heard him mention SynTel. With surprise, she looked up and saw him holding his hand out to her. Automatically, she placed hers in it, and he drew her to his side.

Forcing herself to concentrate, she realized in despair that while she had been entertaining herself she had missed the point of his comments, because *nothing* he was saying made sense.

"Tonight you have all met the woman who has turned our company upside down. She promises, however, to bring order out of chaos—to make us better than ever."

He glanced down at her with a look of pure challenge. Her internal alarm was sounding as she waited for his next words.

He continued smoothly. "As my wife, she has promised to do the same for me. Ladies and gentlemen, please welcome the future Mrs. York Donovan."

Chapter Nine

Tracy's gasp was lost in the rustle of movement and the wave of pleased murmurs that swept the room. York turned to her, raised her left hand and slid a blazing solitaire diamond, roughly the size of the Kohinoor, on her finger. She was vaguely aware of Marcus rising and offering a toast, of the swell of voices and the smiles directed at them.

There was a look of pure devilment, and something else, in York's eyes as he bent his head to kiss her. Before their lips met, he murmured, "Now's your chance, honey. You can tell me to go to hell and create a sensation that won't die down for days."

She didn't have the nerve to cause such a ruckus, and he knew it. Or did he? As their lips met, she intuitively identified his other expression. Uncertainty. Did he honestly believe she was capable of getting her revenge in such a public way? Obviously, he didn't know, but he was gambler enough to take the chance.

For some inexplicable reason that she would have to clear up later, she did not want York diminished in any way. She might rage against his arrogance, but she rejected the thought of him treating her with diffidence. Her lips clung softly, and she raised her hands lightly to his thick hair in tacit reassurance.

She gave a soft sigh of pleasure as her lashes rose and she met his gaze. His eyes blazed with a masculine triumph that left her breathless. Was she crazy? she demanded of herself, her softer feelings vanishing at his look of blatant satisfaction. This man had never had an uncertain bone in his body. Her eyes narrowed in contemplation, but before she could marshal her thoughts, York whisked her out onto the dance floor. They drifted through a series of sentimental tunes. Once, when Tracy tried to speak, York's lips softly touched hers, effectively silencing her. "Not now," he murmured. "I promise we'll talk the whole thing over, but not now."

Content, at least for the moment, to take what the gods were offering, she relaxed, enjoying his taut strength, letting him take over completely. Following his lead was a simple matter. For such a large man, he moved lightly and guided her with assurance, so she simply rested her head on his shoulder and lazily enjoyed the feel of his body.

All too soon it was over. York steered her off the floor and into a small anteroom. She blinked up at him, her eyes wide.

Smiling at her confusion, he said, "You look like an owl." He softly touched her lips with his and pulled her close. "A sleepy owl."

"I'm not so sleepy that I can't talk," she said, tugging at his arms and stepping back. "Why did you do it?" The words hung in the air as he just stood there taking in her dress, her hair, her face.

"York!" She shifted uneasily beneath the curious look of proprietary pleasure on his face. Nervously twisting the ring—not yet *your* ring, one part of her mind noted—she reminded him, "You said we would talk."

"When you walked in tonight, I took one look at you in that dress and wanted to lock you up somewhere where no man could look at you."

"*You* certainly did."

"But you're mine," he said simply.

"That's what we're going to talk about, remember?"

"And the rest of the evening, I didn't get to enjoy the total effect because you were so close to me."

"I noticed," she said dryly, her fingers still toying with the ring.

He reached out to still her hands, slowly nudging the ring back in place with his thumb. He drew her closer, brushing the hair back from her cheeks. "In an hour, I have to be on a plane for England," he said abruptly.

"Damn it, York, I won't have it! You put this great, whacking ring on my finger in front of a million people, then calmly announce that you're leaving the country. Do you realize I hardly even *know* you? You drop in, commandeer me for a couple of days, then disappear. You come back in a week or so and do the same thing all over again.

"You turn my life upside down, and for what? Am I just another challenge in your life? Is this your way of winning? I've found myself in some weird situations before, but this beats them all! You're driving me absolutely crazy!"

"Are you through now?" he asked evenly.

"Only until I catch my breath!"

"Then listen to me while you're breathing. I would like nothing more than to stay with you tonight, to take you home and make love to you all through the night. But I can't. Negotiations for the merger have been resumed, and I have a responsibility to too many people not to be there."

He placed a finger over her lips as they parted. "You're storing up air so you can blast me again, remember? I don't want my father taking you home tonight, but he is. I don't want to get in that damn plane without you, but I will. And you're right. We don't know each other as well as we should, but we will. And soon. When I get back, we'll be together for as long as it takes to get this all straightened out. No more trips, no interruptions, I promise you that."

His hands rested on her shoulders as he finished. "I don't know when I'll be back. Three days, four, maybe a week. But you can believe it will be as soon as I can make it."

"All right," she grumbled in frustration. "We'd better go back in there so you can leave."

"In a minute." Raising her chin with his thumbs, he said, "You talk about going crazy. Honey, you don't know the half of it!" His hand, pressing against her nape, urged her slowly to him. His eyes grew greener at the drowsy look of expectation on her face. Their bodies fused in a heated embrace that muted the distant music and sounds of revelry until there was nothing left but the two of them.

Tracy felt his heart pound against hers as he lifted her. She melted against him as he deepened the kiss. His lips were hard against hers, demanding, urging, draining, drawing from her feelings she hardly knew she possessed. Her arms curved around his neck as she shuddered against him.

"I don't want you to go," she whispered, her lips touching his neck, admitting what her body had already confessed.

"God knows, I don't want to," he said, his hands dropping to her hips, her waist and lightly caressing her breasts.

"Oh, York!" The cry was a helpless appeal for relief, and remorsefully he pulled her to him, soothing her with long, stroking movements until the tremors no longer shook her body. Finally, reluctantly, she pulled away. "You've got to go," she said practically, not meeting his eyes.

Her hands were still at his shoulders, and a sudden blaze of light from her ring drew her attention. "Oh, my heavens! What am I supposed to do with this ring?"

"Don't you like it?" he asked, startled at the turn of conversation.

"*Like* it? I'd have to be insane not to. You may be driving me crazy, but I'm not that far gone," she assured him. "That's the whole problem. It's so beautiful. It's a walking invitation to a thief. What if I lose it, what if—"

"It's insured," he said carelessly. "Promise me you won't take it off." She nodded, and he squeezed her shoulders. "Come on, I'll take you back to the table."

"Oh, no," she wailed softly. "I can't go back like this. I must look awful."

York looked down at her lips, softly swollen by his, and her untamed hair. Her eyes still held the look of a woman who had been well and truly kissed. "You look just right," he said briefly, absorbing the image that would sustain him for the next week.

He returned her to the table, said a few quiet words to his father and the others and left without looking back. Watching the broad-shouldered man walk away from her, Tracy was overwhelmed with loneliness and uncertainty.

Startled by the touch of Meg's hand on hers, she looked up; she nodded affirmatively when Meg asked if she wanted to leave. Marcus smoothed the way and got them to the car with a minimum of fuss. The drive home was quiet. Tracy sat in the back thinking of York, remembering the touch of his lips, his hands, barely aware of the quiet conversation between the two in front.

When they got home, she said an absentminded good night, trailed upstairs and closed her bedroom door. After hanging up her clothes automatically, she followed her nighttime ritual of washing her face and brushing her teeth.

The numbed sense of detachment that had enveloped her for the past hour or so was beginning to fade. She sat on the bed, waggling her hand back and forth, watching the dazzling flash of the ring. It was not just *any* ring, she reminded herself. It was a declaration, a proclamation.

Without a "by your leave" or a "will you please," he had announced their engagement. And she had let him get away with it. He said they would talk when he returned. But how did you tell a man that an enormous ring and a beautiful house and all the money in the world weren't enough? That you needed love and trust?

A wide yawn surprised her. Turning out the lights and sliding into bed, she remembered the philosophy of her favorite romantic character. "I'll worry about that tomorrow," she promised aloud.

The next day was gray and dreary, full of fall's promise and winter's threat. It fulfilled all weather predictions by misting, drizzling, showering and sprinkling. Then, for variety, it drenched, poured, sheeted and flooded. Tracy's mood reflected the weather. She did justice to the previous night's promise by rising to new heights of agitation; she worried magnificently.

First, there was the weather. After all, she was a native Californian. By choice these last several years, she had resided in the southern section, known round the world for its balmy, if occasionally damp, winters. Staring gloomily out of the kitchen windows, she recalled snatches of news items about New England winters. The main ingredients seemed to be snow, ice, below-zero temperatures and wind. If she stayed in this part of the country, the spring thaw would probably find her under a ten-foot snow drift.

And then there was her job. She loved working with computers. She loved the chance to use her ability and knowledge to solve problems no one else could handle. She could no more live the life of a social butterfly than she could focus her entire attention on home and hearth. Visions of silvery-eyed, pugnacious little boys suddenly drifted through her mind. If they were anything like York, they would be a handful. An unexpected, wild surge of desire to bear his children weakened her knees. Plopping down on the sofa, she muttered, "Surely there must be some way to work it out. Other women manage to work and raise a family."

Then, aside from the fact that she would be turning her life upside down, there was his money. There was probably no end to the damned stuff; everything he touched seemed to prosper and turn to gold. Fortunately, his home was that lovely old place with Martha to boss and bully him, instead of a mansion with a retinue of servants.

It was no secret that his first marriage had been a bitter and expensive experience. He was willing to try again, yet he was as suspicious as a wolf sniffing around a well-baited trap. Could she live with such wariness, the feeling of constantly being on trial? Maybe. Did she want to? No.

Prowling restlessly through the empty house, Tracy passed her aunt's bedroom door. If there was a bright spot in this benighted Sunday afternoon, it was to be found in Meg's situation. She had opened Tracy's door that morning, armed with two cups of coffee and a determined expression.

"Rise and shine! It's almost nine thirty, and we've got to be ready in an hour." Meg placed the cups on the bedside table and ruthlessly pulled back the covers until she had Tracy's attention.

"I'm not going anywhere," Tracy said calmly, yanking back the blanket as she sat up and propped a pillow behind her. "But thank you for the coffee."

"Tracy, you've got to come! Marcus is taking us out to his house on the Cape," Meg said, a hunted look in her eyes.

Tracy laughed delightedly. "No way, lady. You've been thoroughly entertained by my running battle with York. It's time you had an undiluted dose of a Donovan male. Don't worry, though, I'll wait up so you can tell me all about it."

Eyes rounded in horror, Meg said, "You're not going to desert me at a time like this, are you? I don't even know the man!"

"It's a terrific way to get acquainted," Tracy said callously.

"What will we talk about? What will I say?" Meg asked, sounding for all the world like a nervous teenager setting out on her first date.

"If the idea upsets you so much, why did you agree to go? You could have said no."

Meg finally broke the thoughtful silence. "He didn't ask me," she said in surprise. "As he walked out the

door, he just announced that he would be here to pick
us up."

Tracy sipped her coffee, looking contemplative. "I
wonder if it's in the genes or environment?"

"What?"

"The annoying manner in which the Donovan men
sweep aside the polite amenities—like asking a
woman if she wants to do something." Sliding beneath
the covers once more, she murmured, "I'll be interested in your opinion, when you know Marcus better." The covers were eventually arranged to her
satisfaction, cocooned around her. "Tell Marcus I'll
take a rain check. No doubt he'll be devastated, but
I'm sure he'll manage just fine without me."

The next morning Tracy knew what she would do
about York's money. As had happened to her so often
in the past when plagued with a persistent problem,
her subconscious had taken over. While she was
stretching like a sleek cat, not yet fully awake, she was
vaguely aware of a lack of tension, of a feeling of
contentment washing over her. Of course! She sat up
with a jerk. How obvious. And how very simple.

As soon as she arrived at work, she looked for
Mary. After discussing the dinner, the surprise an-
nouncement and her new status, Tracy asked abruptly, "Mary, which one of York's legal team handles his
personal business?"

"You mean his will, things like that?" At Tracy's
nod, she said, "That would be Greg Tanner. He went
to college with York."

"I think I remember meeting him," Tracy murmured. "Tall, with sandy hair?"

"That's the one."

"Could I have his telephone number, please?"

"Of course." Concern warmed her voice. "But is
there something I can do? Is anything the matter?"

"On the contrary." Tracy grinned, satisfaction lightening her expression. "Things couldn't be better." A few minutes later, she dialed a number, had a brief conversation and slowly hung up the telephone.

That afternoon at four thirty, she was ushered into Greg Tanner's office. The decor, she decided with an inward smile, was conservative legal with a dash of panache—brown leather chairs, a large, impressive desk, leather-bound books and unexpected splashes of color. A brilliant oil painting hung on one wall, a mosaic dominated another.

Greg was undoubtedly an excellent attorney. Of course he would be; York would have only the best. After a few minutes of conversation designed to put Tracy at ease, Greg smiled and said, "You're obviously here for a reason. What can I do for you?"

"I want you to draw up a prenuptial agreement," she said calmly, observing the look of sharp distaste spreading across his face.

"I am *York's* lawyer," he reminded her, his warm voice slowly icing around the edges.

"That's exactly why I'm here," she stated. Had she not been so determined, the heavy weight of his disapproval would have deterred her. "Please." She smiled appealingly into suddenly cold gray eyes. "Hear me out. I've never done anything like this before, and I can see I'm botching it up."

His face was stiff with reservation as she groped for words. "Oh, Greg, don't be an idiot," she finally blurted in exasperation. "If I was trying to do York out of his money, do you think I would come to one of his best friends? I'm trying to protect him, not scalp him!"

Slowly unbending, he said finally, "Suppose you tell me exactly what you want. I'll even listen this time," he added with a faint grin at the flash of anger in her eyes.

Her words came haltingly as she thought. "I know about York's first marriage and what it did to him. He wants to marry me for any number of reasons . . . but trust isn't very high on the list. I can understand it, I can even sympathize with it, but it would put an awful strain on our marriage."

"I can comprehend that," he said slowly, "but what do you want me to do?"

"I want you to draw up a document, and make it tight as a drum, protecting his interests. I want you to say that if . . . our marriage ever . . . ends in divorce, annulment or legal separation, I would neither ask for, nor receive, any money from him. I would ask for no alimony or support of any kind." Her voice wavered and she blinked two bright eyes, but her expression was one of absolute determination.

"Tracy! I couldn't do anything like that! York would kill me, and make it a mighty slow death, if I interfered in his affairs like that."

"*Please*, Greg. You're the only one I can ask." At his look of stubborn resistance, she almost gave up. Her next words were wrenched out in despair. "York has the money to buy anything in the world he desires. He can do anything, go anywhere he wants. He'll be bringing that to our marriage and sharing it all with me. But he will always wonder if I'll be there waiting when he gets home, or if, someday, he will receive a letter from a lawyer informing him that I want a divorce and half of his earthly possessions."

Her voice wobbling, she asked huskily, "Do you know what it does to a person to always be on the receiving end? Can you imagine what it will be like to marry someone who already has everything? I can't buy him gifts to show him that I care. He has more than he can ever use. Do you know what I have to offer him? Just what you see sitting across the desk from you."

She blinked, forcing back the tears that were threatening to drop at any moment, and cleared her throat. "I thought I had found something he really needed. I thought I could give him back his trust. That was going to be my gift." Her next words were an angry whisper as she wiped away tears with the back of her hand.

"Oh, hell and damnation! I wasn't going to do anything like this." She sniffed as she rummaged through her purse for a tissue. Blotting her cheeks, she looked at the man behind the desk. Her lips moved in an attempt at a smile. "I'm sorry, Greg. I've made a fool of myself, and I've embarrassed you." She rose swiftly, heading for the door. "I shouldn't have asked you. Please forgive me."

She almost collided with him as he reached the door ahead of her, barring the way. His long arm slid around her shoulder, turning her around. "Come back and sit down," he directed gently. "We've got some talking to do."

"Oh, please," she laughed brokenly, "don't be nice to me. I can't handle sympathy when I'm feeling sorry for myself." Obedient to the pressure on her arm, she sank back into the chair. It seemed forever before she could compose herself enough to look up.

Greg was perched on the corner of his desk. He sucked in a deep breath as he looked down into the hazel eyes drenched in misery. "Tracy Maguire," he said slowly, "you tear the heart right out of a man. York is an idiot if he needs a piece of paper to show him what he's getting in you. And I have never had reason to suspect his sanity." He squeezed her shoulder, rose and paced back and forth as he thought. "But if it's what *you* need, I'll do it for you."

He grinned as her face suddenly shone with hope. "On one condition. That you never tell him I did it. If he ever asks, just say you went to the best lawyer in Boston. A deal?"

"A deal," she agreed. "Oh, Greg, I could hug you!"

She wondered how she had ever thought his eyes hard as they laughed down at her. "I don't think my wife would approve, and I know damn well that York wouldn't. I'll settle for a kiss at the wedding."

"I'll leave my address with your secretary so you can bill me," she said as he accompanied her to the door.

"Consider it a wedding present."

The next few days passed—that was the best that could be said for them. Tracy was busier than ever, but the challenge, the pizzazz, was gone. She was waiting. Even though the main frame had arrived and the concurrent demands taxed her energy and ingenuity, she was waiting. It was disconcerting suddenly to feel like a rudderless ship. After twenty-five years of meeting life head on, she was waiting for the return of one man to give direction to her life.

Friday morning, as she stepped out of the elevator, she knew that something was wrong. There was nothing concrete on which to base her fears, but she had learned long ago to listen to her instincts when they slid cold, warning fingers along her nerves. One look at Mary's grim face affirmed her fears.

"York?" she gasped, revealing more than she knew by the one, terror-stricken word.

"No, thank God, but it's bad enough. There was a fire last night."

"In the computer room?" Tracy held her breath, forgetting the alarm and sophisticated gas protective system, momentarily visualizing rampant destruction.

"No. In accounting. And it couldn't have come at a

worse time. The merger went through last night and—"

When Tracy heard those magic words, she lost track of whatever Mary was explaining. York would be coming home! At last this awful uncertainty, this feeling of being only half alive, would be over.

"Tracy! Have you heard a thing I said?" Mary asked with understandable impatience.

"Ah, no . . . I . . . I'm sorry," she apologized, coming back to earth with a bump. Forcing herself to concentrate, she said, "I'm with you now. Tell me again, please."

"Late yesterday afternoon York called Max to request some data, about a ton of it. Max and his crew worked into the wee hours last night. When they were so tired they couldn't see straight, they went home for a few hours sleep. They left everything out so they could come in this morning and dig right in."

"How did the fire start?"

"Who knows?" She sighed wearily. "Could have been a cigarette. Probably was. The fire really didn't get that much of a hold; what did all the damage was the water. If anyone asks," she added dryly, "the sprinkler system works fine."

"I bet Max is fit to be tied."

"That's putting it mildly. Every paper he needs is either stuck together with a hundred others in a sodden mess or disintegrated."

Mary watched in fascination as a seraphic smile slowly curved Tracy's lips. "Somehow I don't think you're taking this with the seriousness it warrants."

"I'm going down to see Max," Tracy decided.

"Why?" Mary asked suspiciously.

"I just want to let him know that all is not lost," Tracy said innocently.

"Tracy," Mary replied firmly, "I hate to be the one

to tell you this, but in case you haven't figured it out, you are not Max Degner's favorite person. If you go down there right now, particularly with that smirk on your face, he's liable to slice you into little pieces with a very dull knife."

Tracy laughed softly. "Mary, he doesn't know it yet, but he's going to love me, smirk and all!"

A few minutes later, after a quick call to Jon, Tracy was on her way down to accounting. Mary had not exaggerated, she realized, as she opened the door on a beehive of activity. Two fire inspectors wandered around, peering and prodding; the maintenance crew stood by, ready to produce miracles as soon as they got the word. About ten department staffers were bent on salvaging what they could, looking with despair at the sodden masses of material. And everyone wanted to talk with Max Degner.

Tracy wound her way through the mess and stood quietly while first one person, then another, vied for his attention. At one point, his eyes lifted, looked right through her, and returned to the person at hand. Deciding, as she had once before, that the spoils did not drop in the laps of the courteous at Donovan's, she raised her voice.

"Mr. Degner." It sounded unusually loud and rather abrupt in one of those momentary lulls that happen even in the most crowded rooms. If she had wanted attention before, she now had an abundance of it. Every eye in the room turned in her direction.

"Could I see you for a minute?" If looks could kill, she thought, I'd be stretched out flat on the nearest desk with a red pencil through my heart.

"You might have noticed that I'm busy right now." His deep voice rumbled to the furthest corners of the room.

"Yes," she nodded agreeably, "and I'm sorry to

interrupt, but I have a message for you from Mr. Donovan." Forcing her eyes to meet his without a flicker, she knew that he knew she was lying.

"What is it?"

"I'm sorry, but it's private. And urgent," she prodded, deciding to give him a little of his own treatment.

"In there," he grunted, pointing to his office. He closed the door behind them, waved her to a seat with a hamlike hand and dropped heavily into a large swivel chair behind his desk. "All right, girlie, you got your privacy. What do you want?"

His personality, she decided, went from surly to snarling and back again without encountering an ounce of charm along the way. "I have no message from York. I lied," she said evenly. "I'm sorry, but I needed to talk with you."

"I knew that. You're a rotten liar. Besides, York wouldn't send a curly-headed kid to me with a message. If he wants me, he talks to me."

What a charmer! She was within an inch of telling him to go back and wring out a few more ledgers! Taking a firm grip on her emotions, she reminded herself how she would feel right now if the damage had been in the computer area. Softening, she thought optimistically that maybe there was a nice man somewhere under that crusty exterior.

"Well?" he prodded. "What the hell is so important that you took me away from that mess out there?"

"I can help you," she said simply.

"Oh, great." He snorted. "The kid with the fancy machines is going to solve all my problems for me."

"Mr. Degner," she gritted through her teeth, "you are a very difficult man to be nice to."

"'Nice' never cut any mustard, girlie. Just tell me what you want."

"I don't *want,* I'm here to give. I have all your accounts, your entire department on magnetic tape."

"How the hell did you do that?" he interrupted.

"Remember the three keypunchers who earned combat pay every time they walked through your doors? That's how. Anyway, it's all recorded, and you can get all the information you need for York on nice, neat printouts from my fancy machines."

"Well," he said moodily, "why don't you go punch a button and get it for me. Or why didn't you just bring it to me instead of coming in to brag about what you can do?"

"I wasn't—" she began, when suddenly she realized what he was really saying. Here was another skeptic, convinced he would be passed by in the progressive world of automation, and fighting every step of the way. Deliberately she studied the man before her. He was brilliant, or at least judged so by those who should know. He undoubtedly was, she acknowledged, if he could keep pace with the business world with his outmoded equipment.

"I can't do it without you," she said simply. Ignoring his start of surprise, she said, "My machines are unbeatable at storing and retrieving information. But someone has to tell them what information to recall, and at the moment, you are the only one who can do that."

"I don't know how to work that thing."

"*I* do," she reminded him gently. "And we have a hotshot programmer who has set up a program. But you are the one who knows what information is needed and how it should be set up."

"I'll be damned," he muttered.

"Our computer isn't ready to run yet, but I've found a compatible one we can use tonight, starting at eight. We'll probably be working for most of the night, but we can't do a thing unless you either supply us with a precise list of your requirements or come along with us. It will be better, of course, if you're there."

The room was silent as he mulled over what she had said. Tracy hesitated to interrupt, he looked so thoughtful, but she could wait no longer. "Is York staying in England until he gets the data?"

"No," he said absently. "He may be on his way home already. I'm going over to work with their accountants. Of course I'll be there tonight," he said, suddenly changing the subject. "What exactly do you need from me?"

"A specific list of what you want. The various ways you need things listed. Do you want the accounts in alphabetical order, listed in divisions, new accounts by year, things like that?" For the next twenty minutes they discussed the specifics, ending as they agreed to meet at eight that evening. Her new partner reminded Tracy of a battle horse, pawing the ground, ready to charge at the sound of a battle cry.

"Anything else?" he asked as she turned to the door.

"Yes." She stopped, directing a level look at him. "My name is Tracy Maguire. You may call me Tracy, or Miss Maguire, whichever you are most comfortable with. But I will not work all night with you calling me girlie."

His awkward grin startled her. "My name is Max, Tracy. And I'm sorry I haven't been very—"

She returned his grin with a brilliant smile. "Don't be sloppy, Max. 'Nice' never cut any mustard!" She closed the door on his roar of laughter.

Chapter Ten

"What in God's name is he doing in there?" Jon inquired plaintively as Tracy sat nursing her latest cup of strong black coffee. He was staring indignantly into the inner office, where Max was hunched over a terminal, pecking at the keyboard.

Belatedly covering a wide yawn with one hand, Tracy slid down in the chair and propped her feet on Jon's desk. Crossing them at the ankles, she said, "I made the mistake of showing him how to formulate queries to request specific data. Before I knew it, he swept me aside, and he's been making like the mad scientist ever since. Terry"—she indicated the tired programmer with a nod of her head—"is keeping him on the straight and narrow."

She studied Jon affectionately. He was crumpled bonelessly in his chair, feet propped on the other corner of his desk. It was almost three thirty, and he had been with them all night. Nice man, she thought for the millionth time, wondering why she couldn't have fallen in love with him. Or at least someone like him, nice and uncomplicated. She ignored the inner voice that dryly reminded her that she had done just that . . . and had been so bored she ended the engagement.

"You saved our lives tonight, Jon," she said with a tired smile. "Thank you."

"Think nothing of it, girlie," he said gruffly, mimicking Max. "What are friends for? How's your hand?" he asked in a different voice.

She examined the swollen knuckles of her left hand, which were now a delicate shade of mauve. "It'll be okay," she said briefly, flexing her stiff fingers. "It's been a long time since I've slammed a door on my hand. I guess I won't be taking *this* off for a while," she commented, touching her ring and setting off a display of light.

"Were you planning to?" His voice was noncommittal, masking his concern.

"I don't know. . . . I don't think so. . . . No, I guess not."

"You don't sound too sure." He sat up slowly. "It's not too late to change your mind. Come on, honey, tell your big brother all about it." She frowned absently at her Styrofoam cup as he said quietly, "It happened awfully fast."

"Too fast," she agreed. "We don't know much about each other, except that we both go up like fireworks on the Fourth of July when we're together. But we will," she promised. "He'll be home soon and we'll talk. We have a lot to settle before I'll know whether or not the ring stays on."

"York might have something to say about that."

"York has something to say about *everything,* but this is one decision that *I* will make."

"Well, call me if you need to be rescued," he offered lightly.

She smiled. "I'll do that, big brother. Lord, but I'm tired! I think the two of them can handle the rest of this. Why don't we go home and get some sleep?"

"Thank God tomorrow, or rather today, is Saturday. I'm going to sleep the whole weekend!" Jon vowed as he stood up.

Tracy stepped into the other room and asked the two men if the program was running smoothly.

"I had to make another slight modification a while ago, but it seems okay now," Terry said, his pale blue eyes never leaving the monitor. Max grunted, an abrupt, but amiable, sound.

"We'll be leaving then," Tracy said, raising her voice over the staccato clatter of the printer. She received a nod from Terry and another grunt from Max.

As she walked into the parking area with Jon, Tracy chuckled drowsily.

"What's so funny?"

"Max's noises are beginning to sound like conversation. If I'm around him much longer, I'll probably end up mumbling and grunting along with him."

"He's been working at it a long time," Jon retorted lazily as they reached her car. "Don't expect to catch up with him right away." Opening her door, he smiled down at her. "You really do look wiped out, honey." He bent his head and dropped a soft kiss on the tip of her nose. "Drive carefully."

Tracy wrapped her arms around his waist in a quick hug and reached up to kiss him on the cheek. "You, too," she mumbled. "Thanks again."

It was fortunate, she thought later, that the traffic was light, because the small part of her mind that was working was not on the road. *York is coming home*, was the melody that sang through her blood. Her internal automatic pilot stopped her at red lights and maneuvered her from one lane to another and finally to the narrower suburban streets leading to Meg's house.

Bone-deep fatigue etched shadows beneath her eyes and drained much of her color, but her eyes brightened as she thought of York. He would be pleased and impressed by what they had accomplished tonight. She could hardly wait for him to see what her sterile, 2001 machine had produced. That should shake his Neanderthal attitude a bit!

Pulling up in front of Meg's garage, she turned off the ignition, leaned back and closed her eyes. She didn't notice the black car parked at the curb. She got out of her car and moved slowly toward the back door. Meg, as usual, had left the outside lights on, so she had no trouble fitting her key in the lock. All that was keeping her moving, she decided, was the thought of climbing the stairs and dropping on her bed.

"Where have you been, Tracy?" The deep voice was level, all but expressionless.

It didn't startle or frighten her; it was almost a continuation of her thoughts. He had come. *He was here!* "York!" She whirled, her face and voice radiant with love.

"It's after four, Tracy. Where in hell have you been?"

Her lips remained curved, like a smile painted on a doll's face. It took a moment to absorb the menace of his quiet stance, to feel the rage emanating from him in waves that reached out, drawing her into a lethal undertow.

"For the third and last time, where have you been?" he rapped out. As she hesitated, adjusting to the change in mood, he asked in an ominously quiet voice, "Have you been with Trent?"

"Yes." Her temper was soaring to meet his. He

expected to hear that she had been unfaithful, seemed to want proof. So be it! She would not apologize for innocence, nor make excuses for long hours of work.

"Did he kiss you?" he snarled, examining her tired face. "Did you kiss him, hold him in your arms?" The words were cold and hurtful, hitting her like pelted stones.

She wondered dully if their chaste little pecks and her impulsive hug would meet York's expectations. It didn't matter. He was in no mood for explanations, and she simply didn't care. "Yes, yes, and yes," she replied evenly. "Is there anything else you want to know?"

"Yes, by God, there is! Did he have the good sense to appreciate what you learned in my arms? You were willing and loaded with potential when I got my hands on you, but very raw material!"

She flinched as if she had been knifed. The warm blood seemed to drain from her body, leaving in its wake a piercing cold that shuddered through her in deep, wracking waves. His warm laughter, the warmer kisses he pressed on her body and the words he had whispered, making her blush all over, had they meant nothing to him? Could he have been untouched by the very things that turned her into a living flame? Apparently so, she decided in anguish. All the dreams she had spun this last week were exactly that, insubstantial wisps that had just been dissipated with a few heartless words.

Drawing a deep breath, she managed a faint laugh. "You know how it is with us virgins, we have to learn somewhere. I'm sorry you had such a rough time of it." Only her eyes gave her away. As she met his in a fleeting glance, they were old and devastated.

"Tracy?" He shook his head as if brushing away a nightmare. His voice was startled, questioning. One large hand lifted, as if to warm itself in her hair.

"No!" Her voice was a terrified whisper. "Don't touch me!" She stiffened against the door and felt it swing open behind her. "Funny," she said bleakly, "I was so tired. But now, more than anything, I need a shower. I feel so dirty." Before the last word was uttered, she slipped inside and locked the heavy door.

As she walked away, she heard York call to her. "Tracy, for God's sake, come back. I didn't—" The words became a stream of savage oaths and a series of muffled thuds. She walked carefully up the stairs, as if one misstep would shred her rigid control. It was a long time before York's car snarled down the street.

He'll be back, some still-functioning part of her mind informed her. First thing in the morning, he'll be back. Ten minutes later, with a bag packed and a note left for Meg saying simply that she had to get away for a few days, Tracy closed the car door and eased out of the driveway. Instinctively, she headed west. West was California and warmth, comfort and love. West was home. Sleep had all but claimed her by the time she was on the outskirts of Worcester. It's a hell of a long way from California, she told herself, but it's a start.

Registering in a motel several miles off the main road, she fell into bed and slept for almost twenty-four hours. Hunger woke her up. Burying her head under the pillow did not soothe her rumbling stomach. Mechanically, she threw on some jeans and a sweater and brushed her hair. Walking back toward the office where she had noticed some dispensing machines, she bought some corn chips, a candy bar and a coke. It was not the most wholesome of meals, but it assuaged the hunger pangs. Shedding her clothes again, she crawled back under the covers and slept until noon.

The whir of the air conditioner sounded loud in the small room. Tracy reluctantly edged away from the numbing depths of sleep. She was curled in a tight ball, her hand beneath her cheek. A dull pain in that region was relieved when she turned her head. Her bruised hand ached and her cheek hurt where her ring had dug into it. She looked at the ring. Her stomach knotted as jagged flickers of nausea passed through her.

Maybe it's just hunger, she rationalized as she slowly uncurled, forcing her taut muscles to relax. Her stomach rebelled at the thought, but she reminded herself that it had been more than a day since she had eaten anything worth mentioning. Slowly climbing back into her jeans and sweater, she shuddered as she looked at her reflection in the bathroom mirror. She blotted the lipstick that resembled a bright gash on her white face, made arrangements in the office to remain another day and asked directions to the nearest restaurant.

The food could have been delicious or horrendous, she didn't notice. While she ate, she coolly arranged her next two tasks. She was unnaturally detached— frozen—but that was all right, she reasoned. It was better than caring. It was better than hurting.

After paying her bill, she returned to her car and drove until she found a telephone booth. Meg answered the phone on the first ring.

"Tracy? Oh, thank God! Are you all right?"

"Of course I am," she said calmly. "I left you a note."

"I know, but York told me what happened. I've been so worried, and *he* is acting like a madman. He's been calling the police and—"

"He probably wants his ring back. Tell him not to fear, I'll get it to him."

"You know that's not true!" Meg began reprovingly, then abruptly changed the subject. "Where are you?"

"I don't know."

"You don't *know!* Tracy, are you sure you're all right? How can you not know where you are?"

"I'm staying in a motel a few miles east of Worcester," she explained patiently, "but I'm at a phone booth in town right now and I—" Her explanation was interrupted by York's deep voice. It was controlled, almost colorless with restraint.

"Tracy? I have to talk to you."

She gently replaced the receiver and left the booth.

One more bit of business to attend to and then she could return to the motel. Spotting a jewelry store, she pulled over to the curb and parked her car. Five minutes later she drove away, ignoring the rapidly fading pressure mark on her ring finger.

Food had not solved the problem of her churning stomach, she acknowledged, as she locked the door behind her and dropped onto the bed. Nerves, tension, call it what you want—it was awful. Tiny tremors shook her body. Reaction, she told herself, gritting her teeth and swallowing convulsively.

Three hours later she was awakened from a light doze by a demanding thunder at the door. Stumbling across the room, she turned the knob and looked up into York's fiercely worried eyes. Her poor, abused stomach gave one final surge of rebellion and Tracy turned, dashing for the bathroom. Throughout the next few ghastly minutes, she was aware of York at her side, holding her head, murmuring soothing sounds. Afterward he washed her face and hands and helped her into a warm robe. His face was as white as hers when he led her back into the outer room.

He propped some pillows against the headboard and settled her against them before pulling a chair next to the bed and easing down into it. Tracy looked at her hands, forcing them to stillness, and wished he would look somewhere else.

"How are you?" he asked gently.

"Fine," she said in a subdued whisper.

"You look like hell."

"I'm okay," she said stubbornly.

The silence in the room was pressing against her, penetrating the brittle shell she had erected around her. Her eyes searched the room restlessly.

"What are you looking for?"

"My purse." It would have been simpler to use a paid messenger or the mail service, but now that was clearly impossible. Anyway, everything else had been difficult with this man, so why should the final severance be any different?

He reached out, snagged the pocketbook off the floor, and dropped it in her lap. She felt in one section, then another, her heart pounding in sudden panic until her fingers closed around the familiar shape. Placing the ring carefully on the arm of his chair, she said quietly, "I'm sorry about the band."

He ignored both her statement and the ring as he gently captured her wrist. "What the hell have you done to your hand?" His eyes examined the bruises in concern.

"Nothing serious. Just a minor confrontation with a closing door." She wiggled her wrist and felt his indecision before he released it.

Their eyes dropped to the ring, its broken band, snapped so easily by the jeweler's tool, a mute testament to the frailty of their bond. A muscle jerked in York's cheek, but his voice was smoothly controlled. "I hope you don't think you're going to shed me as easily as you did that ring."

"It's done," she said calmly, disregarding his determined words. Closing her eyes, she sought the serenity that she needed. She was not disturbed by the man beside her, who watched her with quiet desperation, visibly restraining himself. Gradually, her taut muscles relaxed, faint color returned to her cheeks, and she leaned back against the headboard with a sigh.

"I'm not leaving until we talk," he said finally, breaking the long silence. His eyes brightened at the look of irritation that drew her brows together in a frown. Anything was better than the still, white features set in mute rejection. "I know you'd rather run than face something unpleasant," he goaded deliberately, "but—"

She opened her eyes, then narrowed them. "Are you daring to call me a coward because I have the good sense to walk away from you and refuse to listen to your insults?"

"Yes." He twisted the knife a bit more. "And because you don't have the guts to tell me what your body declares whenever we're within a hundred feet of each other. That you want me!"

"Want you? *Want* you! Listen to me, you arrogant oaf, the only thing I want right now is to watch you walk out that door! Do you hear me?"

"I do," he said dryly. "And I imagine the people who occupy the rooms on either side do too."

"Good! Maybe they'll call the manager. When he comes, I'll tell him that you're annoying me and have him throw you out."

"When I mention that you're my runaway wife, he'll leave us alone."

"I'm not your wife!"

"Not yet. But now that I have your attention, that's what we're going to talk about."

She glared at him in frustration, aware that he had accomplished exactly what he set out to do. "I am not going to marry you," she said, attempting to end the conversation before he could tie her up in knots. "Not now, not in the near future, not ever!"

"Why not?" he asked quietly.

"I can't believe you're even asking. All we ever do is fight! All right, all right," she admitted quickly with an upheld hand, forestalling his comments, "there have been a few times when we haven't."

"Any other reasons?" he asked in a mildly polite tone.

"Plenty! You're too rich, too suspicious, and have a nasty disposition. I don't want to spend the rest of my life dodging verbal bullets."

"Anything else?"

She watched suspiciously as he leaned back at ease, stretching his long legs before him, crossing them at the ankles. "Yes. You do outrageous things, and you disappear for weeks at a time. Because of our stupid bargain, I've been at your beck and call, but if I hadn't, you would have had some other woman in your life. So why should I be crazy enough to marry you?"

"Because, my argumentative little love," he said with a twisted smile, "I don't think I can live without you."

She stared at him, blinking away quick tears. "Don't call me that," she whispered. "You want me, you always have. But don't dress it up with meaningless words." Before he could respond, she asked with sudden curiosity, "How did you find me?"

"You told Meg approximately where you were. After you hung up on me, I started driving in this direction. It took awhile, but I spotted your car, checked in the office, and knocked on the door." He dismissed the trip with a shrug of his shoulders, not mentioning the stabbing anxiety that had accompanied him, the fear that she would be gone before he arrived. He reached in his jacket pocket. "I almost forgot. Meg sent this. Said it might be important."

Tracy accepted the bulky, plain white envelope. Glancing at it briefly, long enough to confirm that it was the agreement drawn up by Greg, she dropped it beside her on the bed, ignoring York's curious glance. It was too late for that now.

"Now, my love," he said deliberately, "if your curiosity is satisfied, may we get back to the point of discussion?" He stood up, moving restlessly around the small room. "First, though, the other night. I said some damnable things to you. They were unjustified and inexcusable, but I hope all the same that you'll forgive me." He returned to his chair, reaching for her hand, hungry for the feel of her.

Regret darkened his eyes as he tried to explain. "I worked sixteen hours a day so I could get back here to you. I knew we had a lot of talking to do, but most of all, I just wanted to be with you. I got to your house about midnight, saw that your car wasn't there and decided to wait. I sweated it out in that car for *four hours!*" He sounded as if it had been four days.

"One minute I was sure you had been in an accident, the next, that you were with another man. Then I'd think of the crazy way I've been acting, and couldn't blame you if you were." Tracy could feel his tension, the effort it took to keep his voice level. "I had just decided that I would kill the man who touched you, when you drove up."

His grip tightened, squeezing her fingers, and Tracy was grateful that he was holding her right hand. His voice was tight with regret as he said, "You got the backlash of the four worst hours of my life. Tracy, I know I don't deserve it for the rotten things I said, but will you please accept my apology and forgive me?" She saw the flash of naked pain in his eyes before his lashes lowered, breaking the connection.

"You're lucky that I have such a rotten temper," she said lightly in an attempt to ease the tension. "I know what it is to say things impulsively and later wish them unsaid." Her voice became quietly formal as she said, "Yes, I accept your apology and yes, I forgive you."

"Thank you," he said quietly, raising her hands to his lips and kissing them lightly. He dropped an extra kiss on her bruised fingers as he said again, "Thank you." He sat back, studying her. "I think we've managed to dispel the anger, but we've got a long way to go before we get back to where we were, haven't we?"

Tracy drew in a deep breath. Might as well get it over with, she decided. No sense in dragging it out. Her voice was calm, quiet. "I don't think we are ever going back. We're just going to have to accept the fact that it won't work for us." She stopped his words with an upraised hand. "No, it's my turn now.

"From the very beginning, you've waited for me to show my true colors. You've expected me to do two things: to get my greedy hands on your money, and to sleep with other men. I'm not that way, but I can't seem to convince you. And I'm not going to spend my life with a man who believes that all women are avaricious little bitches who sleep with every man in sight."

She glanced at his face, knowing he was girding himself for battle behind that blank expression. "While you were gone, I gave it a lot of thought. I finally decided that if the money thing was resolved, the rest would fall in place." She slowly picked up the envelope beside her and offered it to him. "This is how naive and desperate I was."

He withdrew the paper with a questioning look. Shock jolted through his body as he read it. When he finished, he crumpled it up in a tight ball and dropped it on the floor. Tracy wanted to throw her arms around him to absorb the pain radiating from him.

"I haven't done many things in my life that I've been been ashamed of," he said heavily, "but it seems

I've hurt you enough in these last few weeks to spread through eternity. It was bad enough to insult you and extinguish the light from those beautiful eyes, but this," he paused, unable to finish, brushing the envelope off his lap as though it were contaminated.

"How could you have done it?" he asked, searching for words. "How could you have humbled yourself to do such a thing?" He looked at her with too-bright eyes as he said thickly, "I never wanted to diminish you into something yielding and submissive. I want you the way I first saw you, sassy and feisty, raising hell and keeping me in my place. If this is what I do to you, then you're better off without me."

The utter hopelessness of his voice was devastating. Tracy shocked herself and terrified York by crumpling into a ball of misery. Sobs shook her slender form as he eased down beside her and drew her into his arms. The heat of his body seeped into hers and her tears drew to a hiccuping, shuddering stop.

"My love," he murmured in a shaken voice, "my dearest love." The words flowed over in a soft litany of hope. He wiped her tears away, allowed her to attend to a sniffly nose and pulled her back into his arms. She snuggled against him, fitting to the curve of his body.

"Am I your love?" she asked dreamily.

"Now and forever. Through this world and into the next."

When her breathing steadied, he propped himself on a bent elbow, looking down at her. His fingers lingered on her damp face as he brushed her hair back, smoothing it in place. "If we're going to salvage our future," he reminded her gently, "we have to get a few more things behind us."

She inched away, sitting cross-legged, facing him. "I can't think, much less discuss something rationally, in your arms." He waited patiently. "I have to work," she stated contentiously, as if she expected him to handcuff her to the bedpost.

"Good! It's nice to know I'll have someone to support me in my old age." He chuckled at her surprise. "I have enough companies to keep you busy for the next few years. After that, if you want to start a family, we will. When you're ready to work again, we'll arrange it. Believe me, sweetheart, that's no problem. What's next?"

"It's probably going to sound stupid, but I don't know if I can handle the extreme temperatures here. Your winters scare me."

"I'll keep you warm," he promised with a grin. "And when you get too hot, I'll cool you off." At her dubious look, he became serious. "I don't have to be based here. We can live in California part of the year, if that's what you want. Or, if you want to try it here, any time you get too cold, we can get on a plane and follow the sun."

She nodded acceptingly. "Fair enough." The silence that followed was long enough to be awkward. Tracy reviewed what she had said with disgust. Who cared about jobs and the weather? Those were not critical issues, and both of them knew it. They were, she admitted, only useful to keep away from the heavy stuff, the real problem. Mentally shrugging her shoulders and deciding to get it over with, she drew in a long, quivering breath and was interrupted by York at his most provoking.

"Don't tell me that my dauntless little redhead has cold feet?"

She looked into eyes full of tender understanding and . . . what? Determination, resolution? Yes, they were both there, combined with a bit of Irish stubbornness. He would go through the process, his patience would be unending, but he would not admit defeat. How could one man pull so many conflicting emotions from her when she had, for so many years, emerged unscathed from the various lures and traps? Never had she struggled so to remain in control, and never had she been so perpetually off balance.

"All right," she sighed. "You know what it is. It's all that damned money of yours. It's doing two things to us. If I married you . . ." She hesitated, then forged on, ignoring his muttered *"when, not if."* "Everytime we disagreed or argued, you would wonder why I married you and how long I intended to stick around. I want my marriage to last for a lifetime, and with a foundation like that, I can't even see it holding together for a year."

He reached out, gently muffling her discouraged words with his hand. "It's not as bad as all that. Let me try to explain why I've acted like such an idiot with you." He sat up, drew her to him until her head rested on his shoulder, and leaned back against the headboard. Tracy could see the thoughtful expression on his face in the dresser mirror, opposite the bed. He absentmindedly smoothed his thumb across her lower lip, making it difficult for her to concentrate when he finally spoke.

"Ever since I've been old enough to understand what was going on, I've been listed in magazine articles naming the country's wealthy men and eligible bachelors. I've been hunted, pursued, tricked and trapped. All for my money. When I married Amanda, I thought all that was behind me. But she was no different, only a better actress. By the time I realized that her only interest in me was my money, she had a string of lovers all over the city."

His voice was level, as if he were relating a slightly dull story to a distant audience. But Tracy felt the tension in his body and hated the unknown Amanda with an intensity that stunned her. At the same time, she could not believe that this man, who left a trail of women quivering in his wake, could believe their interest was only mercenary.

"The first time I met you, I felt as though someone had hit me over the head with a sledgehammer. I had three thoughts, and each one told me my life was going to change with a vengeance. The first"—he grinned down as she wiggled, agog with curiosity—"was that the next time I saw you, I hoped it would be in my bed. The second was that you had the most honest eyes I had ever seen, and the third, that I was going to make you mine in the shortest time possible."

"Then why—"

"Unfortunately," he overrode her question, "you didn't seem a bit interested in my plans for you. You had entirely too many of your own. Even after our, uh, arrangement, you just seemed intent on killing yourself. You were driving me *nuts!* And, because you didn't feel the way I did"—he squeezed her in remorse—"I said things that I knew weren't true, things that hurt you."

"Will it always be that way?" she asked in a small voice. "Will I pay Amanda's debts for the rest of my life?"

He scooped her up in strong arms, cradling her in his lap. With her ear against his chest, she listened to his rumbling voice. "No," he said absolutely. "You have a sure cure for that. But first tell me the rest of it."

She backed away, supporting herself with a hand on his shoulder, so she could look at him. "The other part has to do with me," she admitted. "Maybe it's misplaced pride, but I'm not good at taking things from people." She ignored his sudden frown. "In any other marriage, I would be able to make a contribution of some sort. It would be a joint effort. But you," she looked at him with somber eyes, "can have anything you'll ever want or need. One-sided arrangements don't work very well."

He gathered her back against him with an audible sigh of relief. "That's where you're dead wrong. What I have a lot of is money and property. But they don't mean one damn thing unless I have someone to share them with, someone to love . . . someone who loves me. You're right, I can buy anything I want. But you are the only one who can give me what I *need*. Just tell me that you love me." He tensed as she leaned back to look into his face. "If you say it, I'll know that you love me for myself, and for all time."

Can it be as simple, and awesome, as that? Tracy wondered. She doubted until she looked up and met hungry green eyes. Eyes that had driven her crazy with their flashing pride and temper were now anxious and vulnerable. She was reminded of a young boy, with his heart in his eyes, waiting for his world to be made a safe place.

"Tracy," he rasped, "if you do, will you please *say* it!"

"I love you," she said, throwing herself into his arms, knocking him sideways so they fell across the bed. "I love you, I love you, I love you!" The words were caroled in between the kisses she planted on whatever part of his face and neck she could reach. "I love you!"

He rolled over, pinning her down, bringing to a halt her impetuous caresses. He kissed her, a slow, drugging kiss, then nuzzled his face in her warm neck. She felt him shudder as he pulled her against him. "I've been so damned scared," he muttered. "I thought I had lost you, and my last chance of love and laughter."

They lay quietly in each other's arms. Passion

would come later; now it was enough to be close, to feel the song of contentment humming through their weary bodies.

"You're very quiet," he murmured.

"Hush! I'm trying to think of ways to spend some of your money!"

His eyes flew open, meeting her teasing gaze. "*Our* money," he said with a lazy grin. "I just gave you joint custody."

"Well, whoever it belongs to, it's very hard to get rid of," she complained humorously. "Now that I have you, I can't think of a thing I want."

"Furs? Jewels?" he tempted.

"Nope." She waved the suggestion away with a flick of her fingers. "How about airline tickets for the Maguire clan, so they can come to the wedding?"

"Too late," was the laconic response. "I've got a company jet waiting at San Jose for them. As soon as they get the word, they're ready to jump aboard."

"York Donovan! You're doing it again! Taking me for granted."

"Never that," he said deeply, disarming her with sudden tenderness. "I know what I have, and I'll cherish you until my dying day. Besides," he encouraged, "it costs more to do it my way!"

Kissing the tip of her nose, he rolled off the bed and reached for the telephone. He dialed a number, waited a moment, said, "You can let him in the house now," and replaced the receiver.

"What was that all about?" Tracy asked blankly.

"It seems that red hair and quick tempers run in your family, my love. Meg took exception to my treatment of you, booted the Donovans, father and son, out of her house, and said we couldn't return until she knew you were healthy and happy. Dad has been pacing up and down her front porch ever since I left."

He bent over and tossed the crumpled sheets of paper into her lap. "Now, my tiresome little love, see if you can destroy these as easily as you do thousand dollar bills."

As she sat, looking uncertain, his voice revealed his pain. "I *never* meant to have anything like that between us. The day I mentioned my lawyers, I only intended for them to cut the red tape so we could be married right away." He stood over her, unmoving, as she shredded and disposed of the papers.

She slid to her feet, eyeing this man of hers. Fatigue, concern, regret, the residue of the day's anguish were still etched on his face. She couldn't bear it. She wanted him healed and whole. And she didn't intend to be treated like a delicate piece of spun glass for much longer.

Wrapping her arms around his waist, she said softly, "I want you to love me, York."

"Honey, if I loved you any more, I'd probably explode."

"I mean, I want you to make love to me." She felt the shock jolt through him.

"What!"

Color flared in her cheeks and her eyes promised retribution to this dense love of hers. "I know I'm not doing this as well as you could, seeing that I lack your vast experience, but I'm asking *you*"—she tapped his chest with a finger—"to make love to *me,* on *that.*" She waved at the bed.

"Tracy!"

"York Donovan, you've been hell-bent to seduce me since the day we met. Now, when I try it, you look as disapproving as John Calvin witnessing an orgy! Will you please make up your mind!"

Crushing her to him, he laughed joyously. Sobering suddenly, he asked, "Are you sure?"

Her radiant face was answer enough. Even so, she whispered, "Oh, my darling, I need you so."

He reached out and, with agonizing slowness, dealt with the sash of her robe. She shivered at the look on his face as it fell open. With his fingertips, he gently nudged it from her shoulders, his eyes never leaving her as it fell to the floor.

She stood proudly before him, rejoicing that her body could elicit such desire in this man.

"You are so beautiful," he said slowly, huskily, as he lowered his head. His lips were warm on hers before they went lower still and caressed each breast. His hands slid under the band of her bikini pants and traced her curves as he pushed the wisp of lace down to her ankles. Before he stood, his hands raised to her hips, and he leaned forward to kiss the soft curve of her stomach. She sucked in her breath, her muscles contracting at the touch.

He rose, tossed back the covers, lifted Tracy and placed her in the middle of the wide mattress. He tore off his clothes with jerky movements of his hands and joined her. His hands and lips explored and memorized every curve of her body, as she uttered soft, gasping cries.

"York . . . darling?"

"Soon," he promised. "Soon."

A raging summer storm sent lightning forking through her body, creating unbearable tension. Suddenly she was drawn into a dark funnel, spinning higher, darker, tighter, until she cried out for release.

Later, drifting back in large, looping circles, she felt his arms once again. She opened heavy eyes, knowing he had not left her. "My God," she whispered in awe, "is it always like that?"

A somber look of concern lifted from his eyes, and the creases in his cheeks deepened at the beginning of an exultant grin. "No, honey, it isn't. We had the best there is." He held her to him as their heartbeats slowed to normal. Later, and still later again, he reached for her, taking her with him to another time, another place. They fell into an exhausted sleep in the early morning hours.

Waking up in the arms of the man you love is a perfect way to begin the day, was Tracy's first thought the next morning. She sighed, remembering, and looked with utter contentment at the man beneath her. She was half sprawled over York, using his broad chest as a pillow. Her arms were resting loosely on his shoulders, with one slim leg tucked warmly between the two of his.

The even rise and fall of his chest informed her that he was still asleep. Shifting a bit, she propped her elbows on the slabs of muscle above his rib cage, resting her chin in her hands as she gazed down at him. No, not exactly a handsome man, she decided once again. The hard planes of his face were too ruggedly masculine for that. But, whether he was, as now, clad in nothing at all, or in one of his vested business suits, he was sexy as hell, and she could hardly keep her hands off him.

"Well?" he asked suddenly. "Have you come to any decision?"

"About what?" she asked, startled, all but tumbling off her warm perch.

"Whatever. You've been doing some heavy think-ing for the last few minutes."

"Can you see through your eyelids?" she asked with interest.

"Uh-uh," he denied lazily, running his hand with casual intimacy over her bottom and down the back of her thigh. "I could feel it. Every delightful, curvy inch of you was preoccupied."

His hands tightened as she tried to move away. "Come on, give."

"I gave last night," she said, giggling.

"Tracy," he warned, wrapping his arms around her.

"All right, all right. I was planning a wedding. Ours."

He sat up, bringing her with him. "I don't know how much you can manage to do in eight hours, but go to it."

"What are you talking about?"

"I mean that you've driven me crazy long enough. I'm not waiting one more day to put my ring on your finger. At six this evening, we're meeting my family and yours in Las Vegas. By six thirty, we'll be married."

"We can't do that, can we?" she asked as he hustled her into the shower.

"We can."

"So soon?"

"Uh-huh."

"You arranged this?" She gasped as warm water poured over her body.

"One telephone call in about ten minutes will take care of it."

"You seem to be telling, not asking me," she observed.

"Damn right!"

"I won't do it."

"You will," he vowed, rubbing soap on his hands and smoothing it on her body.

And she did.

Silhouette Romance

IT'S YOUR OWN SPECIAL TIME
Contemporary romances for today's women.
Each month, six very special love stories will be yours
from SILHOUETTE.

$1.75 each

☐ 100 Stanford	☐ 128 Hampson	☐ 157 Vitek	☐ 185 Hampson
☐ 101 Hardy	☐ 129 Converse	☐ 158 Reynolds	☐ 186 Howard
☐ 102 Hastings	☐ 130 Hardy	☐ 159 Tracy	☐ 187 Scott
☐ 103 Cork	☐ 131 Stanford	☐ 160 Hampson	☐ 188 Cork
☐ 104 Vitek	☐ 132 Wisdom	☐ 161 Trent	☐ 189 Stephens
☐ 105 Eden	☐ 133 Rowe	☐ 162 Ashby	☐ 190 Hampson
☐ 106 Dailey	☐ 134 Charles	☐ 163 Roberts	☐ 191 Browning
☐ 107 Bright	☐ 135 Logan	☐ 164 Browning	☐ 192 John
☐ 108 Hampson	☐ 136 Hampson	☐ 165 Young	☐ 193 Trent
☐ 109 Vernon	☐ 137 Hunter	☐ 166 Wisdom	☐ 194 Barry
☐ 110 Trent	☐ 138 Wilson	☐ 167 Hunter	☐ 195 Dailey
☐ 111 South	☐ 139 Vitek	☐ 168 Carr	☐ 196 Hampson
☐ 112 Stanford	☐ 140 Erskine	☐ 169 Scott	☐ 197 Summers
☐ 113 Browning	☐ 142 Browning	☐ 170 Ripy	☐ 198 Hunter
☐ 114 Michaels	☐ 143 Roberts	☐ 171 Hill	☐ 199 Roberts
☐ 115 John	☐ 144 Goforth	☐ 172 Browning	☐ 200 Lloyd
☐ 116 Lindley	☐ 145 Hope	☐ 173 Camp	☐ 201 Starr
☐ 117 Scott	☐ 146 Michaels	☐ 174 Sinclair	☐ 202 Hampson
☐ 118 Dailey	☐ 147 Hampson	☐ 175 Jarrett	☐ 203 Browning
☐ 119 Hampson	☐ 148 Cork	☐ 176 Vitek	☐ 204 Carroll
☐ 120 Carroll	☐ 149 Saunders	☐ 177 Dailey	☐ 205 Maxam
☐ 121 Langan	☐ 150 Major	☐ 178 Hampson	☐ 206 Manning
☐ 122 Scofield	☐ 151 Hampson	☐ 179 Beckman	☐ 207 Windham
☐ 123 Sinclair	☐ 152 Halston	☐ 180 Roberts	☐ 208 Halston
☐ 124 Beckman	☐ 153 Dailey	☐ 181 Terrill	☐ 209 LaDame
☐ 125 Bright	☐ 154 Beckman	☐ 182 Clay	☐ 210 Eden
☐ 126 St. George	☐ 155 Hampson	☐ 183 Stanley	☐ 211 Walters
☐ 127 Roberts	☐ 156 Sawyer	☐ 184 Hardy	☐ 212 Young

$1.95 each

☐ 213 Dailey	☐ 217 Vitek	☐ 221 Browning	☐ 225 St. George
☐ 214 Hampson	☐ 218 Hunter	☐ 222 Carroll	☐ 226 Hampson
☐ 215 Roberts	☐ 219 Cork	☐ 223 Summers	☐ 227 Beckman
☐ 216 Saunders	☐ 220 Hampson	☐ 224 Langan	☐ 228 King

Silhouette Romance

$1.95 each

- ☐ 229 Thornton
- ☐ 230 Stevens
- ☐ 231 Dailey
- ☐ 232 Hampson
- ☐ 233 Vernon
- ☐ 234 Smith
- ☐ 235 James
- ☐ 236 Maxam
- ☐ 237 Wilson
- ☐ 238 Cork
- ☐ 239 McKay
- ☐ 240 Hunter
- ☐ 241 Wisdom
- ☐ 242 Brooke
- ☐ 243 Saunders
- ☐ 244 Sinclair
- ☐ 245 Trent
- ☐ 246 Carroll
- ☐ 247 Halldorson
- ☐ 248 St. George
- ☐ 249 Scofield
- ☐ 250 Hampson
- ☐ 251 Wilson
- ☐ 252 Roberts

- ☐ 253 James
- ☐ 254 Palmer
- ☐ 255 Smith
- ☐ 256 Hampson
- ☐ 257 Hunter
- ☐ 258 Ashby
- ☐ 259 English
- ☐ 260 Martin
- ☐ 261 Saunders
- ☐ 262 John
- ☐ 263 Wilson
- ☐ 264 Vine
- ☐ 265 Adams
- ☐ 266 Trent
- ☐ 267 Chase
- ☐ 268 Hunter
- ☐ 269 Smith
- ☐ 270 Camp
- ☐ 271 Allison
- ☐ 272 Forrest
- ☐ 273 Beckman
- ☐ 274 Roberts
- ☐ 275 Browning
- ☐ 276 Vernon

- ☐ 277 Wilson
- ☐ 278 Hunter
- ☐ 279 Ashby
- ☐ 280 Roberts
- ☐ 281 Lovan
- ☐ 282 Halldorson
- ☐ 283 Payne
- ☐ 284 Young
- ☐ 285 Gray
- ☐ 286 Cork
- ☐ 287 Joyce
- ☐ 288 Smith
- ☐ 289 Saunders
- ☐ 290 Hunter
- ☐ 291 McKay
- ☐ 292 Browning
- ☐ 293 Morgan
- ☐ 294 Cockcroft
- ☐ 295 Vernon
- ☐ 296 Paige
- ☐ 297 Young
- ☐ 298 Hunter
- ☐ 299 Roberts
- ☐ 300 Stephens

- ☐ 301 Palmer
- ☐ 302 Smith
- ☐ 303 Langan
- ☐ 304 Cork
- ☐ 305 Browning
- ☐ 306 Gordon
- ☐ 307 Wildman
- ☐ 308 Young
- ☐ 309 Hardy
- ☐ 310 Hunter
- ☐ 311 Gray
- ☐ 312 Vernon
- ☐ 313 Rainville
- ☐ 314 Palmer
- ☐ 315 Smith

- -

SILHOUETTE BOOKS, Department SB/1

1230 Avenue of the Americas
New York, NY 10020

Please send me the books I have checked above. I am enclosing $_____
(please add 75¢ to cover postage and handling. NYS and NYC residents please
add appropriate sales tax). Send check or money order—no cash or C.O.D.'s
please. Allow six weeks for delivery.

NAME _____

ADDRESS _____

CITY _____ STATE/ZIP _____

READERS' COMMENTS ON SILHOUETTE ROMANCES:

"The best time of my day is when I put my children to bed at naptime and sit down to read a Silhouette Romance. Keep up the good work."

P.M.*, Allegan, MI

"I am very fond of the quality of your Silhouette Romances. They are so real. I have tried to read some of the other romances, but I always come back to Silhouette."

C.S., Mechanicsburg, PA

"I feel that Silhouette Books offer a wider choice and/or variety than any of the other romance books available."

R.R., Aberdeen, WA

"I have enjoyed reading Silhouette Romances for many years now. They are light and refreshing. You can always put yourself in the main characters' place, feeling alive and beautiful."

J.M.K., San Antonio, TX

"My boyfriend always teases me about Silhouette Books. He asks me, how's my love life and naturally I say terrific, but I tell him that there is always room for a little more romance from Silhouette."

F.N., Ontario, Canada

*names available on request